Al

The Duke's Wicked Wager ~ Lady Evelyn Evering

CONTENTS

THE DUKE'S DAUGHTER

The Duke's Daughter

Lady Amelia Atherton

Ladies of Bath

Isabella Thorne

A Regency Romance Novel

The Duke's Daughter ~ Lady Amelia Atherton
Ladies of Bath
A Regency Romance Novel

The Duke's Daughter Copyright © 2017 by Isabella Thorne
Cover Art by Mary Lepiane

2017 Mikita Associates Publishing

Published in the United States of America.

www.isabellathorne.com

Part 1

Fate's Design

1

With a few lines of black ink scrawled on cream parchment, her life had changed forever. Lady Amelia had to say goodbye, but she could not bear to. She sat alone in the music room contemplating her future. Outside the others gathered, but here it was quiet. The room was empty apart from the piano, a lacquered ash cabinet she had received as a gift from her father on her twelfth birthday. She touched a key and the middle C echoed like the voice of a dear friend. The bench beneath her was the same one she had used when she begun learning, some ten years ago, and was as familiar to her as her father's armchair was to him.

Lighter patches on the wood floor marked where the room's other furniture had sat for years, perhaps for as long as she had been alive. New furnishings would arrive, sit in different places, make new marks, but she would not be here to see it. Amelia ran her fingers across the keys, not firmly enough to make a sound, but she heard the notes in her head regardless. When all her world was turmoil, music had been a constant comforting presence. Turmoil. Upheaval. Chaos. What was the proper word for her life now?

She breathed in a calming breath, and smoothed her dark skirt, settling it into order. She would survive; she would smile again, but first, she thought, she would play. She would lose herself in the music, this one last time.

TWO WEEKS EARLIER

LADY AMELIA LOOKED the gentleman over. Wealthy, yes, but not enough to make up for his horrid appearance. *That* would take considerably more than mere wealth. He leered at her as though she were a pudding he would like to sample. Though it was obvious he was approaching to ask her to dance, she turned on her heel in an unmistakable gesture and pretended to be in deep conversation with her friends. Refusing the man a dance outright would be gauche, but if her aversion was apparent enough before the man ever asked, it would save them both an embarrassment. She smoothed her rich crimson gown attempting to project disinterest. It was a truly beautiful garment; silk brocade with a lush velvet bodice ornamented with gold and pearl accents.

Lady Charity, one of Amelia's friends in London, smiled, revealing overly large teeth. The expression exaggerated the flaw, but Charity had other attributes.

"That is an earl you just snubbed," said Charity, wide-eyed. It both galled and delighted Lady Charity the way Amelia dismissed gentlemen. Lady Amelia did not approve of the latter, she did not take joy in causing others discomfort. It was a necessity, not a sport.

"Is he still standing there looking surprised?" Amelia asked, twirling one of her golden ringlets back into place with the tip of a slender gloved finger. Looking over her shoulder to see for herself would only confuse the man into thinking she was playing coy. "I am the daughter of a duke, Charity. I need not throw myself at every earl that comes along."

"Thank goodness, or you would have no time for anything else." Charity's comment bore more than a tinge of jealousy.

Lady Amelia's debut earlier this Season had drawn the attention of numerous suitors, and the cards still arrived at her London townhouse in droves. Each time she went out, whether to a ball or to the Park, she was inundated with tireless gentlemen. If she were a less patient woman, it would have become tedious. Gracious as she was, Amelia managed to turn them all down with poise. Lady Amelia's father, the Duke of Ely, was a kind man who doted on his only daughter but paid as little mind to her suitors as Amelia herself; always saying there was plenty of time for such things. Her debut like most aspects of her upbringing was left to the professionals. What do I pay tutors for? He had said, when a younger Amelia had asked him a question on the French verbs. There had been many tutors. Amelia had learned the languages, the arts, the histories, music and needlepoint until she was, by Society's standards, everything a young woman should be. She glanced across the hall to that same father, and found him deep in conversation with several white haired men, no doubt some of the older lords talking politics as they were wont to do. She flashed him a quick smile and he toasted her with his glass.

Father had even indulged her by hiring a composer to teach her the piano, after she proven herself adept and eager to learn. If any of these flapping popinjays were half the man her father was...she thought with irritation.

Lady Patience, the less forward of Lady Amelia's friends, piped in, "Men are drawn to your beauty like moths to a flame." Her voice had a sad quality to it.

"I'm sure you will find the perfect beau, Patience." Amelia replied.

"Yes, well, you might at least toss them our way, when you have decided against them." Charity said. She peeked wide eyed over her silvered fan which covered her bosom with tantalizing art. Amelia's eyes were brought back to her friends and she smiled.

While Charity was blonde and buxom, Patience was diminutive, yet cursed with garish red hair. The wiry, unruly locks had the habit of escaping whatever style her maid attempted, leaving the girl looking a bit like a waif. Although her dress was a lovely celestial blue frock trimmed round the bottom with lace and a white gossamer Polonese long robe joined at the front with rows of satin beading, she still appeared frazzled and misplaced at an elegant ball like the one they were attending.

Charity's flaws were more obvious, apart from her wide mouth. She had a jarring laugh, and wore necklines so low they barely contained her ample bosom. The gown she was wearing extenuated this feature with many rows of white scalloped lace and a rosy pink bodice clasped just underneath. It bordered on vulgar. Amelia intended to make the polite suggestion on their next shopping trip that Lady Charity perhaps should purchase an extra yard of fabric so she might have enough for an *entire* dress.

"Do not be foolish, Patience. You deserve someone wonderful. If we must be married, it should be to someone that... excites us," Amelia said, rising up onto her toes and clasping her hands in front of her breast.

Her comment caused Patience to flush with embarrassment. It was easy to forget Patience was two years older than Amelia and a year older than Charity, for her naivety gave her a childlike demeanor.

"Not all of us are beautiful enough to hold out for someone handsome," said Patience. When she blushed, her freckles blended with the rosiness of her cheeks. Her eyes alighted with hope, and she was pretty in a shy sort of way.

Charity nodded her agreement, but Amelia frowned and clasped Patience's hands. "You are sweet and bright and caring. Any man would be lucky to have you for his wife. Do not settle because you feel you have no choice. The right man will come along. Just you wait and see."

Tears swelled in Patience's bright blue eyes. Amelia hoped she would not begin to cry; the girl was prone to hysterics and leaps of emotion. Charity was only a notch better, and if one girl began the other was certain to follow. Two crying girls was not the spectacle Amelia hoped to make at a ball. She clapped her hands together and twirled around, so her skirts fanned out around her feet.

"Come now; let us find some of those handsome men to dance with. It should not be hard for three young ladies like us." Amelia glanced back. Patience was wiping at her eyes and fidgeting with her dress— no matter how many times Amelia scolded her for it, the girl could not quit the nervous and irritating gesture—which generally wrinkled her dress with two fist sized wads on either side of her waist. Meanwhile Charity was puffing out her chest like a seabird. One more deep breath and she was sure to burst her seams.

It would be up to Amelia, then. In a matter of minutes she had snagged two gentlemen and placed one with Charity and one with Patience on the promise that she herself would dance with them afterward. Though men waited around her, looking hopefully in her direction, none dared approach until she gave them a sign of interest. She had already earned a reputation of being discerning with whom she favored, and no man wanted the stigma of having been turned away. Amelia perused the ballroom at her leisure, silently wishing for something more than doters and flatterers after her father's influence.

SAMUEL BERESFORD DID NOT WANT to be here. He found balls a tremendous waste of time, the dancing and the flirting and, thinly veiled beneath it all, the bargaining.

For that was what marriage boiled down to, a bargain. It was all about striking a deal where each person involved believed they had the advantage over the other. If it were not for his brother's pleading, he would never be seen at a fancy affair like this. Dressed in his naval uniform, a blue coat with gold epaulets and trimmings and white waistcoat and breeches, he attracted more attention than he wished.

"Stop scowling, Samuel," said Percival as he returned to his brother's side from a brief sojourn with a group of lords. "You look positively dour."

"Did you find the man?" Samuel inquired.

Percival sipped his wine and shook his head. "It is no matter. Let us concentrate on the women. We should be enjoying their company and you seem intent on scaring them all off with your sour expression."

Unlike himself, Samuel's older brother Percival loved the frivolity of these occasions. As the eldest son of an earl it was very nearly an obligation of his office to enjoy them, so Samuel could not begrudge his brother doing his duty.

"You think it my expression and not our looks that are to blame?" Samuel asked, only half in jest. To appease his brother he hid his scowl behind the rim of his wine glass.

The Beresford brothers were not of disagreeable appearance, but they lacked the boyish looks so favored at the moment. They did not look gentlemanly, the brothers were too large, their features too distinctly masculine, for the women to fawn and coo over. Additionally Samuel had been sent to the Royal Naval Academy at the age of twelve, a life that had led him to be solidly built, broad across the chest and shoulders. He felt a giant amongst the gentry.

"Smile a bit brother, and let us find out." Percy elbowed Samuel in the side.

"What is a wife but an ornament to show off at these functions? I cannot imagine any necessary criteria other than beauty. Just pick the prettiest one and have done with it." Samuel's comment earned him a narrow-eyed glare from a passing woman. He smiled gaily back at her.

"How can I when my brother insists on offending them before I can open my mouth? I should have left you at home," Percy said with a long suffering sigh.

"I wish you would have done."

Samuel did not mind life ashore in small doses. It was a chance to have a real meal, something other than salt-cured meat, and a decent cup of tea with fresh cream. He also got to spend time with Percy, though he would not admit to missing his brother out loud. After too long on land, however, he become irritated and itched to get back to his ship, until it became a near-physical pain to be away from it.

"Father insisted you interact with women whose company you did not pay for." Percy said as he sipped from his wine glass.

"I heard him threatening to reduce your allowance. Do you think you could survive on your officer's stipend?"

"I could," Samuel said peevishly.

"Besides, I have missed you, dear brother and if I did not drag you along with me I would never get to see you," said Percy. "No doubt you will be back at sea before the week is out."

Until the time Samuel had joined the Royal Navy and left home, he and his brother had been nigh inseparable. Only a year separated them in age, but the lives they led could not have been more different. Samuel had long ago banished any remnants of jealousy he had once felt at his brother's status, something earned with nothing more than the luck of being born first, and Samuel would no more trade places with Percy than he would with a beggar on the street.

"I shall be a good little brother then and assist you in your hunt for a wife," said Samuel. "After all it is essential that the heir get an heir. I myself am not so encumbered." He swapped his empty glass for a full one and walked in a lazy circle around the room, his brother in tow.

"First, we must find the most beautiful woman in the room. No, not her, that is for certain. Did you see the ears on that one? I could use them for wings and fly myself to France."

Percy snickered, but turned it into a cough behind his hand. "Really now Samuel, stop insulting them and be serious!"

It was Samuel's opinion that Percy would benefit from considerably less seriousness in his life. He already bore the marks of stress and duty in the frown lines beside his mouth and even a few strands of grey had appeared in his dark hair.

"Fine, fine," said Samuel, coming to a halt. He never felt quite steady on solid ground and was always bracing himself for the rocking of a deck. "There. She is the one."

Samuel pointed. Percy swatted his hand down and looked around anxiously. "Do not go pointing like you have seen something you wish to buy in a shop window. These sorts of women do not appreciate being treated so. And no, certainly not her," Percival hissed.

Percival was being obstinate. The woman was clearly the most lovely in the room by a fair margin. She had hair the color of warm honey and her gown was a vibrant red, which perfectly complemented the pearly sheen of her skin. Luminescent that is what she was, shining in the light of the chandelier.

"Why not?" Samuel asked, frowning. He squinted, trying to pick out some flaw his brother must be seeing.

"Because she" said Percy, taking Samuel by the arm and drawing him further away from the lady in question, "is Lady Amelia Atherton."

"Lady Amelia? What luck! You do know my ship's name is the *Amelia*, Percy. You cannot count this as anything but fate that you should marry her." Privately, Samuel did not believe in fate, but his brother was a romantic. The sooner he got his brother a bride, the sooner he could quit these ghastly outings.

Percy was gaping at Samuel as if he were a fool. "While you may find that a fine reason to select a wife, it is not a matter of whether or not *I* will have *her*. She is most sought after woman of the Season. Beautiful, wealthy, the daughter of the Duke of Ely I shall just step in line behind her hundred other suitors, shall I?"

Though Percy had lived a charmed life, he had never acquired the arrogance or confidence of some of his peers, to his detriment.

"Do not step in line behind them, dear brother. March to the front. Women like a little brashness."

"How many drinks have you had, Samuel? It would do nothing but embarrass me to treat my peers rudely."

"Damn. Why would you care what they think?"

"I am in Lords with the lot of them. I won't make enemies without cause. No, pick another, any other," Percy insisted. He had gone a little pale, as if the mere thought of asking Lady Amelia Atherton for anything at all horrified him.

"This is all a bit absurd, do you not think, Percival? You are a man grown. She is hardly more than a girl. The right mix of good looks and bravado would have her melting in your arms," Samuel argued. "I cannot believe you are being unmanned by a girl of what, eight and ten?"

"Do you see the swarm of men about her? Men who have tried, and failed, to do just as you seem to think I should do with ease. Count me out, Samuel," said Percy. "Besides, having a wife quite so beautiful is asking for a lifetime of headaches."

Samuel had no firsthand experience with wives, but he could not imagine handling one was any more challenging than handling a ship. Spirited, willful, but under the right command, pliable and eager to serve. He told Percy as much.

"Oh really, *Commander?*" said Percy, brow furrowed in the way that meant he was trying to hold back laughter. "If you are so skilled at 'taming the willful seas' let us see you manage a single dance out of her."

"Me?" said Samuel, poking himself in the chest. "I have no desire for a wife."

"But if you demonstrate these skills, perhaps I can

learn from you. Go on now, what are you frightened of? For a man with your looks and... what was it, bravado? She should be sweet butter in your hands."

The challenge held little appeal for Samuel. She was pleasing to look at, but he would get nothing more from her than a dance, which was hardly worth his while. Still, if it would demonstrate to his insecure brother than confidence was the crux of the matter, it would be worth it.

"Fine," said Samuel at last. He drained his glass and handed it off to Percy. With a hand through his already disheveled locks, he said, "Watch and learn, brother; though she will be ruined for you, once she has met me."

"Samuel, you cannot," Percy argued looking for a place to set down the two glasses he now held. "You are not introduced." He took a long suffering breath as if steeling himself. "Come, I will introduce you."

"You will not; you will ruin everything," Samuel said as he headed straight for the woman.

PERCY STOOD OPEN MOUTHED, but watched with avid interest and not-quite-hidden horror as Samuel marched over to the Lady Amelia Atherton. She was turned away at the moment, conversing with another gentleman. Samuel stepped up beside her, a step closer than the other man, just inside the amount of space considered polite, and the other man quite naturally backed up. Her hazel eyes flashed, and Percival half-expected her to slap his brother.

"Dear God man, you are boring the woman to death; can you not see that? Now run along," Samuel said, waving a dismissive hand at the fellow.

The man's look of outrage and befuddlement was quite the show, and Percival could barely keep from laughing aloud. He turned away a moment to compose himself, and when he turned back, his brother was bowing over the unfathomable Lady Amelia Atherton's hand. She had a look of bemusement on her face, her lips turned up in a slight smirk. Percival wondered just how long it would be until his brother was turned away with the same callousness that he had shown the previous man; although the next time, Percy supposed the dismissing would be done by the Lady Amelia.

2

It was not the rudeness of the man that intrigued Lady Amelia, though that was part of it, she supposed. Nor was it his appearance, which was aggressively masculine from the strong prominence of his nose to the ferocity of his brow. She generally liked finer men, but he was amusing. If she had to pinpoint what it was about him that persuaded her to accept his offer of a dance, it was that he gave her no opportunity to say no. He seemed to assume she would say yes, and because he could imagine no reason for her refusal, she was forced to agree. It did help the man's appeal that he had sent the doddering Lord Cornishe on his way, and his hand was very warm under his glove...warm and large, she thought.

She almost regretted her choice when the dance began. The man, whom she did not know though she knew every peer by face and name, was not a grand dancer. He was barely passable.

"Have you never danced the quadrille before?" Amelia asked. She could guess his answer.

Samuel shook his head, and his coffee-colored eyes were intense with concentration. "Not much call for dancing on a ship, quadrilles or not."

That would explain why she did not know of him. Her memorized list of men worth knowing did not extend to military or naval officers. They were fine husbands for girls like Patience, but the daughter of a duke had no need to marry a second son.

"You are a captain?" Amelia had no difficulty carrying on a conversation while dancing. The steps were as natural to her as were the chords on a piano.

"A commander," said Samuel.

Lud, she thought as she moved through the steps.

"Commander Samuel Beresford," he said. "Go ahead, laugh at my dancing, I can see that you want to. I will not take offense."

"Truly," she teased. "Men take offense at the slightest affront, I've found."

Lady Amelia Atherton, was dancing with a naval commander! Oh, Amelia could just imagine the talk. It would be a delicious morsel of gossip by morning but despite the man's worst efforts, she did not mind dancing with him.

"It is dreadful, but at least you are aware of that. So many men believe themselves to be the best at something, not realizing they are making fools of themselves," said Amelia. "But I will not mock you. At least you are trying to better yourself. You are trying, are you not?"

"I think I have got it now," said Samuel, as he moved away from her to take the hand of Lady Pottinger and Lord Caney became Amelia's partner.

She had danced with Lord Caney before, but decided against him as a potential suitor. He was handsome enough and wealthy, his coat was bedecked with gold buttons, but there was something about him that seemed disingenuous. His voice was too careful and cultured his hands just a bit too warm and soft. When Lord Caney spoke he made her feel she was missing some great jest at her expense.

Lady Pottinger was shooting Amelia a hateful look behind Samuel's back that said her choice in dance partner was not appreciated.

"I will owe Lady Pottinger an apology now," said Amelia, when Samuel once again took her hand. "And perhaps a small gift. You trod on her toes."

Samuel shrugged his shoulder. There was something appealing about his uniform, with its stark lines and flashy gold accents. "Once or twice, maybe."

"But you have not stepped on mine at all."

"Hmm," said Samuel concentrating.

Amelia looked at him out of the corner of her eye. It was hard to read him, between his height and the positions of the dance.

"Commander Beresford, did you step on her slippers on purpose? You scoundrel," Amelia admonished, but she was laughing inside. Lady Pottinger was on the edge of spinsterhood and acted as if it were the fault of all the young debutantes who ousted her.

Samuel ignored the question. "What did you say to

that man?" he asked, nodding toward Lord Caney. "He is staring at me as if I personally offended him. Though, perhaps I have, but I cannot remember how."

"You have offended him by dancing with me. Do not pay him any mind. I have danced with him before and do not care to repeat the experience," Amelia said.

"Was I not your first?" Samuel asked.

Amelia snapped her head up, but there was no guile on Commander Beresford's face, neither so much as a smirk. Had she imagined the innuendo? Those were not ladylike thoughts to have. She shook her head to clear it and tried to focus on the dance again. But she could not stop herself.

"Am I yours? The first you have danced with tonight, I mean," said Amelia, looking up at him through her lashes. Any other man would have lost his breath or blushed or something but he just looked down at her as if she were nothing more than his dance partner.

"Yes, in fact," he said. There was not so much as a tremor in his voice.

"And how," said Amelia, letting a bit of annoyance creep into her tone, "did I earn that honor? Your dancing is such a gift, Commander Beresford, you should not be so ungenerous with it."

"My brother pointed you out as the most beautiful woman in the entire room. Or was it all of London? England? I cannot remember," said Samuel.

Amelia had heard that before. How dull. Men were capable of no original thought when it came to women or beauty. "Your brother is too kind."

"He is, yes, but that is not the reason I chose to dance with you," said Samuel.

"No?" Amelia bristled at his tone, as if he had deigned to dance with her, and not the other way around.

"No," said Samuel. "Once my brother told me your name I could not resist. It is the same name as my ship's, you see. I wanted to see if you had anything in common with her."

"I beg your pardon," said Amelia, spine stiffening. "Are you comparing me to some barnacled old hunk of wood?"

"Not unfavorably, I assure you."

Lady Amelia had the distinct feeling that she was being made a fool of. And by a nameless man no less. A commander! She pursed her lips and gave Commander Beresford a look that had sent better men than him running. He was either oblivious or fearless, for he stepped back and bowed in the customary ending of the quadrille with a smile on his face, as if he had gained some advantage. Amelia gave him a curtsy, the smallest she could manage, and turned away. Half of her wanted him to follow her and insist on a second dance. The other half was so off balance from his rudeness and, if she were honest with herself, his lack of weakness toward her, that she hoped to never see him again.

Patience and Charity were nowhere in sight. Annoyed, Amelia stalked off to find herself a refreshment. Three separate men accosted her on her way and she was about to allow the third, the least offensive of them, to fetch her a drink, but instead, Lord Caney was again at her side with a glass of punch. "Allow me to offer you refreshment, Lady Amelia," he said, handing her the glass and expecting to speak with her. She wished she could refuse with grace, but the man was much too insistent. Some people just did not understand the meaning of no. She took the glass with a brief thanks and meant to brush by him, but he caught her arm. "That officer is beneath you," he said.

She fluttered her eye lashes at him. "Just because one is a second son, is no need to give him the cut."

She started to pull out of his grip, but he tightened his fingers for just a moment. "Dancing with him, will inspire the gossips," he warned.

"Let them talk," she said flippantly. She wished her friends would hurry back. She wanted to escape Lord Caney's boorish conversation, and more than that, she wanted to tell her friends all about Commander Samuel Beresford and his presumptions.

The girls arrived after the next dance, pushing their way through to Amelia, giggling and red-faced, and she at last managed to escape Lord Caney to meet them.

"You two look as if you have stolen sweet cakes from under your nanny's nose," said Amelia, looking them over. "What has gotten into you?"

The two girls exchanged a look and burst into laughter again. Amelia rolled her fingernails against her glass, impatient and irritated.

"Patience is in love," said Charity, followed by an unseemly snort.

"I am not!" Patience protested. "But he is good looking."

"The man you danced with?" Amelia asked, frowning.

She could not remember who she had set up with Patience. She had never been forgetful before, especially when it came to dancing and suitors.

"No," Charity said. "Just a man she walked by! Can you believe it? Our little Patience is smitten over a man she has not even spoken a word to."

"Oh do not tease me please," Patience begged. "And I am not smitten. I only said that I think he is handsome."

"And you smiled at him," said Charity.

Amelia, whose patience had grown thin after the rudeness of Commander Beresford and the presumptions of Lord Caney, held up a hand to stop their chatter. "Please, can we have a coherent conversation? If I wanted to listen to prattle I would call my suitors back. Who is he?"

"I do not know," said Patience, looking down at her hands. Was she on the verge of crying? "I only passed him and smiled and he smiled back at me."

That was hardly enough to get on with. "I see."

"He looked ill," Charity offered. "Green as a frog and sweating besides. Not exactly a dashing figure."

"Be nice, Charity," Amelia warned. "I am happy for you, Patience. I will endeavor to discover the name of your mystery man."

But what about her mystery man? Nonsense. She shook her head. Samuel Beresford was a nobody. He was not worth thinking about. No matter that he was good looking, plenty of men were that, nor that he had made her feel... what was it that feeling? Excited. Giddy, even. As if they had shared a sort of secret.

"Truly? Thank you, Amelia," said Patience, looking as if she might hug her. Amelia took a half step back.

"But what about that officer you were dancing with?" Charity asked. "I do not recall ever seeing him before. He was handsome was he not? In a brutish sort of way."

Patience giggled.

"He was nobody," said Amelia. "I have already forgotten his name."

It was a lie and she knew it, but no one else needed to.

SAMUEL WATCHED Lady Amelia stalk away. It was not an unbecoming gesture from her, the way her hips and hair swayed back and forth with each step. She seemed quite furious with him. And why should he care? He stuffed his hands into his pockets and took the long way around the room back to his brother, after locating two glasses of brandy. Though he intended to give one to Percy when he found him, one glass was empty by the time he located his brother.

"Well then, I have won the bet," said Samuel. "Are you quite all right? You look ready to cast up your accounts."

Percy was a pale shade that bordered on green, and there was a sheen of sweat across his brow, but he waved away his brother's concern. "Did you...did you offend Lady Amelia Atherton? Please tell me it was not what it looked like."

"I think she was rather charmed by me. Infatuated, even," said Samuel.

"Samuel, I might be rubbish with women but even I

know that making one stomp off the dance floor without a backwards glance is not a good sign. She looked as if she wished to stab you. What did you do?" Percy asked with a grimace.

"She is a spoiled, haughty girl," said Samuel. "I told her the truth and she acted as if she had never heard it in her life. She probably has not. It was good for her, Percy. Do not fret over it. My actions do not reflect upon you. She doesn't even know you are my brother."

Percival rarely acted like an older brother, but he seemed determined to put in a good showing now. He drew himself up in a fair imitation of their father before a lecture. Samuel prepared to tune him out.

"And you, brother, are a spoiled, haughty boy. I know you have nothing but disdain for the world I live in, but to take out your ire on an innocent woman seems a new level of cruelty for you."

"And how am I haughty and spoiled? I have hardly lived the charmed life. I have worked on a ship since I was—"

"Yes, yes," said Percy, and though his face was still sickly pale, splotches of red bloomed on his cheeks. "Since you were twelve years old, I know. You are a hard worker, and so brave, and so very righteous. You look down your nose at everyone who is not on a ship and never cease complaining about the drudgeries of dry land. One doth protest too much, I think."

"Are you implying that I am jealous?" Samuel's voice dropped lower, and he stepped in close to Percy. "That I wish I had your life? Full of parties and gossip and whatever else men with too much time on their hands do?"

Percy deflated under Samuel's glare. It both pleased and saddened Samuel. Yes, he had always enjoyed holding some power over his older brother, but he never wished to see Percy cowed so easily.

Percy rubbed a hand over his face. He could not meet Samuel's eye. "No, no, I did not mean that. I... I do not know what I meant. Forget it, Samuel. I am feeling quite out of sorts. I believe I may have eaten something that does not agree with me."

Samuel wanted to have it out with Percival, in words or, better yet, with fists, but Percy always diffused this sort of thing and he did look ill. It was the lords, Samuel thought. All those old men were sucking the life right out of his brother.

"Fine. Any excuse to leave." Samuel said downing his last finger of brandy while glancing around the room. There she was. Lady Amelia Atherton. She was surrounded by men again, all with foolishly open faces, enthralled by her looks and charm. Her expression was a polite interest, but he could see, despite the space between them, the boredom in her eyes. Eyes which had sparked with fire when he had teased her.

"I have to give my excuses to the hostess," said Percy. He looked about to keel over.

"Really? The fool hostess has fed you something foul and you will thank her for it?"

"Samuel," Percy said. "You are being rude."

"Can you not simply write the excuse tomorrow when you are feeling better?"

"No, Samuel, I cannot."

Samuel sighed and stowed his empty glass in a nearby planter. "I will call the carriage."

Percival's look of disappointment made Samuel's stomach turn with guilt. Well, it was not the first time he had disappointed his brother, and it would not be the last.

3
----

*T*he day was a bleak one. Lady Amelia had woken to a stone grey sky and by the time she had dressed, the rain had begun. It beat against the windows, but she was tucked inside, warm and dry and safe from its touch. Patience and Charity sat on the sofa, sipping tea and nibbling delicate cakes, while Amelia played a meandering tune on the piano.

"Is that a new song?" asked Patience. "I have not heard that one before."

"It is not a song really, not yet. But yes, it is something I am working on," Amelia replied, as she began the tune again. She would not tell them it was inspired by the man she had danced with, a love song to the sea. Why was she thinking of him?

"Is your father home?" Charity glanced around the room as if he might be hiding behind a curtain there.

"No, he is at Westminster today."

"A shame. He is such an interesting man," said Charity.

Amelia's fingers stuttered over the keys. She shot Charity a glare over her shoulder, then went back to playing. "He is. And he is not interested in you."

The idea of her father not only remarrying, but remarrying *Charity* was too horrible to contemplate. She was certain Charity teased her with the idea because she knew how it nettled Amelia, and not because of any real interest.

"But he must be looking for a wife," Charity persisted, as if Amelia's annoyance had not been clear enough. "He has no male heir and he is not growing younger. It has been four years since your mother died. Most men would not have waited so long."

Patience whispered something to Charity, words Amelia could not make out over the sound of her playing. Amelia's mother had died giving birth. She had been pregnant three times before that, and each had ended in tragedy. This fourth had been full of promise, until she had gone into labor. Neither she, nor the baby boy, had survived. A little brother Amelia would never know.

"Would I call you mother, then?" Amelia's tone was ice, but she doubted Charity would pick up on that. The girl knew nothing of subtlety.

"I hope this weather will not hold out," Patience chimed in, her voice strained. "It would put a damper on our trip to Bond Street and I am in desperate need of a new hat. Nothing in my collection goes with the new yellow silk I purchased. My brother was eager to chaperone us, though he insists we be away by four. I told him we would be finished long before then, so we might walk in the park before sunset." She ended with a nervous laugh.

Yellow silk with her pale skin and, that shade of red hair? Amelia grimaced, but she appreciated Patience's effort to steer the conversation toward brighter territory. She was about to suggest perhaps a green instead, but Charity was not to be deterred.

"Surely you would be in your own house with your own husband," said Charity, around what sounded like a mouthful of cake. She would take soft and plump too far, if she were not careful Amelia thought uncharitably, although she would not say so out loud

"I am in no hurry to marry." She replied instead

Charity laughed. "Everyone knows that. What, do you dream of spinsterhood? Living alone in an apartment with your piano? You would die of boredom. There would be no one left to admire you."

"The sooner you marry, the sooner you must provide children. It would be no great thing to you, I imagine, to lose your figure, but it would be a dreadful thing for me," said Amelia, not needing to look to see the indignant hurt on Charity's face. She could say as many terrible things as she liked, but the moment she received one back she would fall apart.

There was a minute of poignant silence, Amelia's hands hovering over the piano keys. She had lost the strand of the music in her mind, the weaving of chords she had been building. With a sigh, she picked up a familiar tune, one of the first she had learned as a child.

"But if you fell in love you would marry, would you

not?" Patience asked pleasantly, seeming oblivious to the barbs Charity and Amelia had flung at each other. No doubt Patience was thinking of the man she had shared a smile with at the ball.

Amelia envied the girl her easy heart, and said a silent prayer that she never lose it.

"Falling in love is beneath our dear, lovely Lady Amelia," said Charity still with a hint of acid.

"Do not be silly. Of course I will marry, as is expected of me. If I wish to postpone it for a while, who can blame me? There is more to the world than a husband, but once you have one, that is all you will get. Best choose a good one."

Charity tutted. "You are frightening Patience. Do not be dissuaded by her bitterness, Patience. A husband and a house are just the beginning. Did you discover anything about the gentleman from the ball?"

Amelia set the cover down on her piano and rose. She paced to the window and drew back the curtain. Still raining. What did one do when it rained at sea she wondered? There was only so much room below decks, she imagined, so did they stand out in the rain, becoming drenched? No, that was silly; they would catch their deaths from cold and fever.

"I have not found out anything yet," Amelia admitted. "But I have plans to meet my Aunt Ebba for tea. She knows everyone, even better than I do. I will take your description to her and then we can tell everyone who the lucky man is."

Patience blanched, and Amelia laughed.

The sounds of a carriage pulling up outside the

townhouse had all three girls up on their feet, craning their necks at the window.

"Father is home," said Amelia.

The Duke of Ely stepped out of the carriage beneath a servant's umbrella and marched to the front door, the servant scurrying to keep up. Amelia, Charity, and Patience hurried out to greet him.

"Good afternoon, ladies," he said, handing off his overcoat. His face was worn and weary. Each time he returned from a session of Parliament, Amelia felt he had aged five years. She feared for him of late. He would never talk about his worries with her, would never unburden himself. "I am not here for long. Just a change of clothes and I am off again. Business to be done, and all that. Did I interrupt your fun?"

"Of course not, Your Grace. This is your home, you can never interrupt," said Charity, edging her way closer to Amelia's father. "I did hope you would join us, your company would be like sunshine on this rainy day."

Amelia caught her father's eye. Charity was truly laying it on thick, and with all of her usual subtlety.

"Thank you for the kind offer, but I am afraid I do not have the time. Perhaps another day. Now, please excuse me," said the Duke of Ely, practically fleeing for the staircase.

Once he had gone, Amelia rounded on Charity. "Pray do not harass my father in his own home. Could he have been more clear? He has no desire for your company. Really Charity, you embarrass yourself, and me."

Charity had the nerve to look offended, her nostrils flaring. "I was being friendly Amelia, perhaps you ought to try it sometime. I am beginning to believe you do not turn suitors away at all, but rather they flee upon realizing what a cruel girl you are beneath the lovely veneer."

Amelia recoiled. Charity may as well have slapped her in the face. "Why are you being so hateful? Are you jealous of me?"

It was the wrong thing to say. Charity turned on her heel and stomped her way back to the parlor where they had been sitting. Amelia and Patience followed, watching her snatch up her shawl from the sofa and fling it about her shoulders. She jabbed a finger at Amelia.

"You think you are so much better than everyone. But a pretty face and the latest fashions do not hide that you are cold, and distant, and you look down your nose at people because you are afraid to let them get to know you. It is pathetic, and weak and no one will ever love you because you will not let them. Now go on, I know what you are thinking, that I am too emotional, too forward, but at least I have emotions! I have passions!" Charity had worked herself into a state, advancing on Amelia until she had backed her up against the sofa.

"Passions," Amelia said. "Lud, Charity."

"Do you know what they say about you, Amelia? They say you are as beautiful as a diamond, and as warm as one. Men want to possess you, because you are the shiniest gem, but they do not want to know you. Someday one of them will propose marriage, but you will still be a bauble on the shelf."

With that, Charity left. She did not wait for a servant to bring her an umbrella or to call her carriage; she let herself out of the house, slamming the door so violently the windows rattled. Patience had a hand cupped over her mouth, eyes wide. Amelia sat down on the sofa. Her legs would not hold another moment. She should have said something. What had she done to deserve such hatred from her friend, and how long had it been simmering beneath the surface?

"You do not need to stay, Patience. I know you must believe those things as well," said Amelia softly.

Patience did not go, however. She sat down beside Amelia, and, after a moment's hesitation, wrapped her arm around Amelia's shoulders. Amelia's father came down the stairs a minute later and poked his head into the parlor.

"What the devil was all that ruckus about?" he asked. He stepped inside the room when he caught sight of Amelia. "Are you all right darling? What is the matter?"

Amelia took a shuddering breath. Just as her father would not unburden himself on her, she would not unburden herself on him.

"Nothing, father. Just a misunderstanding between friends," she said, standing to kiss his weathered cheek. "Please do not be late," she said.

"I cannot promise," the duke said, "After what happened at the ball last night. I fear ..." He broke off and Amelia asked "What happened father?"

Her father smiled wanly, but it did not reach his eyes. "Nothing you need worry about. I will take care of it." He patted Amelia atop her head as if she were a child. "I will not be home for dinner, but perhaps I will see you at breakfast. Buck up, darling, troubles only linger if you let them."

She reached up to straighten her chignon, but his words chilled her. What troubles did he speak of? What did her father fear?

Then he was gone with as much speed but with far less noise than Charity. Amelia sat back down beside Patience. She was creasing her dress in her hands.

"You will ruin your dress if you keep that up," said Amelia.

Patience sniffed.

The patter of rain on the windows rose and ebbed as the wind caught hold of it. Amelia looked out of the window and saw the carriage being brought around. She was glad Charity was not out in the storm and had gone straight home, which for all her drama was just a few doors down. Patience sniffed again.

"What is it?" Amelia asked. "You only make that noise when you have something to say and do not know how to say it."

"I just... well, there was some truth, maybe, in what Charity said. You are hurt, or at least upset by the things she said but instead of talking about it you remind me not to crease my dress," said Patience, still not looking up. She had switched to wringing her hands, but was at least leaving her dress out of it. "I do not think you are cold, but... you do not hold much respect for emotions."

Amelia tried to be reasonable and think about what Patience was saying before dismissing it. "That is not true. I feel... things. I just do not believe that everything I feel needs to be gratuitously expressed. Is that so awful?

Am I a terrible friend because I do not weep or stomp about?"

"Of course not. I do not think you are a terrible friend at all," said Patience, turning to face Amelia. "I think you are a wonderful friend. Charity was quite mean to say the things she did."

Amelia felt a peculiar ringing in her ears. "But you do not think she was wrong. Do you think I will die a spinster too? Alone but for my piano, as she said?"

It was not fair for Amelia to punish Patience with Charity's words, but she could not stop herself. Once she felt this detached, cold anger, there was no staying it. She expected Patience to quail as she normally did, to look away or to leave, but the girl took a deep breath.

"I think you are frightened because of how your mother died, but I do not think it is an unreasonable fear. You are not the first woman to fear it. But I..." Patience winced, but kept on. "I think you use it as an excuse not to get close. If you do not like anyone, you do not need to marry anyone, and so you will not need to go through that ordeal."

Amelia did not want to hear any more. Emotions were threatening her, welling up almost past the point of managing, and she did not want anyone around when they broke through. She stood up, rolled her shoulders back, and fixed a smile on her face.

"Thank you for your honesty, Patience. It seems the rain will not be letting up, and so we will not be able to go shopping, nor to the park. It is a shame," said Amelia with clear dismissal.

Patience looked about to cry, blue eyes watery and

big. "I understand. But I will see you soon, Amelia. I will not let you avoid me."

The girl's resolve, newfound and tremulous, filled Amelia with warm affection despite herself. She saw Patience to the door, with an umbrella and a carriage to hurry into, and waved farewell. Then, alone again, Amelia sat down at the piano.

The wood was smooth beneath her fingers, the metal knobs cold as she lifted the cover. Every emotion she did not want to feel, she poured into her playing. At first the music was loud, chaotic, but the longer she played the more it mellowed, soothing her, until she was again playing the beginnings of her ode to the sea. Likely it would never be properly finished. She had a habit of picking things up and fiddling with them until, frustrated that they would not work quite right, she put them back down and forgot about them.

A talented player, her teacher had told her father, but she will never be a composer. To create, you have to make mistakes, to begin again over and over until it is perfect. She does not have the tolerance for it, the passion. Was it true? Did she lack passion?

Do not take it the wrong way, he had cajoled Amelia, there is nothing wrong with sticking to what you know; it is frightening to put yourself into the music, to see what you are made of. Amelia's cheeks had burned at the criticism and she had never attempted to compose again. Until now.

4

————

*P*ercival's health did not improve. He complained of a burning in his mouth and stomach. By the time they got home, his stomach pain was truly terrible and Samuel had only once seen a sailor in similar pain. He had died from a poisoning from bad fish. Afterwards the doctor had said, if he had purged himself at once with a cup of sea water, he may have cast up the offending matter and lived. When Samuel suggested such a thing to Percival, his brother had said he had been trying not to retch the whole ride home.

Still Samuel fetched him a glass of warm water with salt in it. A single swallow was all Percival needed to rid himself of last night's dinner. Once he started, it seemed he couldn't stop. He woke several times during the night. By early morning, he woke feeling feverish, still complaining of stomach pains, and Samuel had ordered him to stay in bed until the doctor arrived. Samuel had sat at his bedside, speaking of nothing, until Percy fell asleep from sheer exhaustion. Their father, the Earl of Blackburn, had entered the room mid morning.

"How are you feeling, Samuel?" his father asked. "You two ate the same things last night, did you not? And yet Percival is the one who has fallen ill, while you are hale as ever."

It almost sounded as if their father blamed Samuel for being healthy. Almost.

"I feel fine, Father, but I do not know all Percy ate last night. We did not spend every moment together," said Samuel, getting to his feet. He had been sitting on the floor, leaning against the bed, while Percival slept. "I thought it would put a damper on his wife-finding attempts, dragging his younger brother around."

His father laid a hand on Percy's forehead. There was a fondness there, a tenderness, that had never been between Samuel and his father. They were too different. Or too alike.

"Well, the doctor will be here soon. You should not be sulking about when he does, he will need room to work, said Lord Blackburn.

"Wonderful. I will take my sulking elsewhere." Samuel paused in the doorway. "Where is mother, by the way? Still at Stanherd?"

Stanherd Residence was his mother's retreat, a renovated country home with an expansive garden. Lady Blackburn had gone to live there last summer, ostensibly for her health, but had not returned home. It was a sore point for Father, so Samuel enjoyed reminding him of it whenever he had the opportunity.

"No. She is visiting her sister in Bath," his father replied. A muscle in his jaw jumped.

Samuel raised his eyebrows and left the room. He missed his mother. She was the steadying influence in the house, the thing that kept the three men from being at each other's throats. He could not blame her for growing weary of the job. Still, he would have been happier to be home if she had been there to talk to. Crossing the hall, he went to his room. It was sparse, and the only personal touch was the painting on the wall, an oil painting done by his mother of a ship caught in a storm. She had captured it perfectly despite having never been aboard a ship, the forlorn feeling, as if there were nothing in the world but the ocean, the storm, and the vessel itself. The way the ship carried on, despite the waves crashing into it, the rain that deluged the decks and the enormity of the ocean.

He had only been caught in two such storms. The memories were as clear as if they had happened just yesterday, gilded by fear and the rush of joy precipitated by coming out alive. What could compare to that feeling? His brother, his father, they would never understand it. Nor would a wife. Though the Lady Amelia Atherton seemed a tempestuous thing, but he had no doubt there was a placid wife beneath the fire. He would be bored within a week. It was unfair both to her and to him to consider her at all. Why, then, was he thinking of her again?

43

5

---

*A*fter Lady Amelia and her Aunt Ebba breakfasted with the duke, they dressed in their finest walking clothes, and went out to shop. Lady Amelia always adored her Aunt Ebba, she was more like an older sister than an aunt. Aunt Ebba was much younger than her mother, but many people said the sisters had looked and acted alike in spite of their difference in age. Aunt Ebba and her husband Uncle Edward had always been in Lady Amelia's life, along with her ten year old cousin Phillip.

"It is a shame that Patience could not join us," Amelia said. "She was so looking forward to shopping. She sought a new hat to go with her yellow frock. Yellow can you imagine? It washes out her color so much she practically disappears. She is so quiet that there is a danger of her disappearing at any rate."

"Indeed," Aunt Ebba said. "You could take a lesson, Amelia, and be a bit more demure."

Amelia scowled at her.

"Stop that," Aunt Ebba replied. "You will be wrinkled before your time."

Amelia softened her face obediently. "Do you remember the dress? It was a beautiful fabric."

"I don't believe I recall," said Aunt Ebba thoughtfully, "Although, green should be her color, not yellow. Did I see the dress in question?"

"I don't know. It is just the color of the embroidery on the dress you wore to the last ball, albeit, quite a bit less decorative. It is a traveling dress, not a ball gown. I have a bit of fabric cut from the seam. I told her I would look for something."

"You are kind," Aunt Ebba said.

The shop was the place to be seen and the pair were attracting all sorts of attention. Amelia wore a lovely cream walking dress trimmed in pink satin with four puffed flounces along the skirting and Aunt Ebba was in a periwinkle blue ensemble with a contrasting peach shawl. Aunt Ebba was a stylish woman, only fifteen years older than Amelia, and she loved to be seen. Normally, Amelia was happy to take part, but her recent fight with Charity had somewhat spoiled her mood. The girl had not even come around to apologize the next day, and Amelia was not sure what to do when the conversation fell to her dilemma.

"And then she just walked out, right into the rain; slamming the door as if she intended to take it with her. Not so much as a by your leave. Charity can be so churlish," Amelia complained, lightly tossing aside the bonnet the shop clerk was trying to sell her, onto the pile of other discarded hats. "That one is dull. Do you have perhaps any new novelties?"

"We knew that though, the way she displays her assets," Aunt Ebba said. "No decency. Obviously, you are right. She should be the one to apologize, but I cannot refrain from suggesting that you are better off without her friendship. That girl was one step away from a scandal, and you do need to be careful where those are concerned, hmm? You must be above reproach." Aunt Ebba admired a towering purple turban, replete with feathers and flowers in all shades of yellow. It was striking, and just the sort of thing she adored.

Amelia busied herself with scrutinizing yet another hat. "But we have been friends for ages. I do care about her, and I feel as though I am in the wrong," said Amelia.

"Well you are not. The way she chases after your father is disturbing. He has expressed no interest whatsoever. It is shameful."

"At least I have Patience," said Amelia, delicately fitting a dark green bonnet on top of her hair. A delicate spray of golden leaves and tiny pale yellow flowers decorated the brim. "She is a loyal friend. I had hoped you might help me with a favor for her, in fact. What do you think of this for her? Think of this green against her red hair."

"I like it," Aunt Ebba said. "I think it will do splendidly. Those tiny flowers are just right for Patience, and there is little enough yellow so that even if the color is not completely correct, it should do nicely with her yellow traveling dress."

Amelia set the bonnet in the pile of things she

planned to purchase. It was not a statement piece, but a sensible bonnet that would suit many occasions. It was just right for Patience. "And one other favor," Amelia said.

"Of course," said Aunt Ebba, tossing the purple turban on top of the pile with a wink. "What can I do?"

Amelia glanced around. The clerk was no more than ten feet away, searching his supply for suitable offerings. She did not want to seem common, asking about a man, nor did she want rumors to begin about Patience's feelings for him.

"The other night we were at a ball and she saw, in passing, a man she took a liking to. He left in a hurry, though, and we were unable to catch his name. You know how she is, mooning after him because he smiled at her." Amelia shrugged politely.

If Aunt Ebba had ears, they would have perked at that. There was nothing the woman enjoyed more than budding romance. She, a married woman, insisted that she lived vicariously through those stories of love and infatuation and kept up with all of the gossip as a means of enriching her life.

"Do tell. What did he look like?" Aunt Ebba waved the clerk away when he approached with a tower of hat boxes. He set them down, wobbling, on the table and left them alone.

"Well, he was quite ill it seems, and left in a rush, but he was tall, well above most anyone else there, and his features were exaggerated. Or so Patience said. I did not see him myself but I imagine a large nose and eyebrows and ears or something of the sort. He had dark hair and was well-dressed but not like a dandy. It is not much to go on but that is all we have." Amelia was not hopeful. It was a thin lead, even for her aunt.

But Aunt Ebba looked very pleased with herself and a knowing smile dimpled one of her cheeks.

"What?" Amelia prompted. "You know something, what is it?"

"Oh this is a delight, Amelia, you do not know?"

Amelia sighed. She hated these games, but her aunt delighted in them. Being begged for information was almost as pleasurable as acquiring it.

"No, I do not. Please, tell me. Who is he?" If Amelia had any inkling on her own, she would have refused to ask on principle, but she did want to help Patience.

Like a cat with a fresh bowl of cream, Aunt Ebba savored the moment. "Do you know there is a bit of gossip floating around about that ball? In particular, about you?"

Amelia's stomach clenched. She flashed back the entire evening, trying to think of what she could have done to start gossip. Her thoughts went to the young commander and she flushed prettily.

"I did not know that," said Amelia at last. "Is Charity spreading some sort of lie about me? I would not put it past her."

But Aunt Ebba shook her head. "I have this from a reliable source. You were seen dancing, and enjoying yourself, with a nobody of a man. Some military man, they said. That you were giggling and smiling and flirting with him, as you have done with no other man. Someone has cracked the diamond, they claim."

Amelia closed her mouth with a snap. It had fallen

open as her Aunt had gone on, when she realized what sort of foolish sop people believed.

"Hardly. I gave him a single dance because I was bored and he was amusing, if only for his awful dancing. Really, people can be so absurd. If I smiled at him, it was because he had made of himself as a jester does. It is hardly declaring my intent to marry the man. I cannot even recall his name."

Samuel Beresford. She did remember it but she refused to acknowledge that out loud. A commander, not even a captain. It was ludicrous.

"But you should!" cried Aunt Ebba, clapping her hands in delight. "You should, because the man Lady Patience is so smitten with is that man's brother."

Amelia had no response to that. Her mouth had fallen open again and, she realized with great annoyance, that she was twisting her skirts between her hands, like Patience. She brushed irritably at the wrinkles.

"Yes, I can see you hadn't the slightest idea. Mm, the Beresford brothers. Sons of the Earl of Blackburn. The elder brother, Percival Beresford is known to be shy, a bit of a recluse, but handsome and gentle. The younger, Samuel, is hardly known at all, apart from his good looks and his fondness for light skirts," said Aunt Ebba, as casually as if they were discussing a game of cricket.

"He was not *that* good looking," said Amelia, lamely.

"Of course not, dear."

By THE TIME they returned to Aunt Ebba's townhouse

they accrued quite a pile of packages. Over half were Amelia's, and she sent the man on to her home when he had finished unpacking, but stayed for tea with Aunt Ebba. She had not gotten over the shocking news from the hat shop, and was still debating whether or not she should tell Patience the truth.

"But why not? The son of an Earl is a more than fine match for her," said Aunt Ebba, biting into a crunchy biscuit.

"It would be awkward. If she married him then I would be thrown together with the younger brother on all sorts of occasions, and with these rumors flying about..." Amelia had no stomach for sweets at the moment. She took a long sip of bitter tea.

"No doubt the younger Beresford will be back at sea soon," Aunt Ebba said.

A servant pushed into the room. He carried a note on a silver tray, which he gave to Aunt Ebba. She looked down at it as she was about to set it aside, frowned, and tore it open. Her face paled. Amelia could see her fingers shaking, until the note slipped free and floated down to the carpet, face up.

"Auntie? What is it?" Amelia stooped down to pick up the note and hand it back, but she saw something in the black ink that caught her eye. *Terrible accident.* "W-what has happened?"

But Amelia read it for herself. Words and phrases jumped out, as if her mind were incapable of reading it as a coherent message.

"Oh no," Aunt Ebba began, cut off by a sob. "Your

father, I mean. Oh Amelia do not read the details, please."

But it was too late. *Carriage accident. Dead on impact. Grievous wounds. Dead on impact.* She had not even had a chance to say goodbye. Amelia felt her knees give way beneath her and she collapsed to the floor. Tears did not come at first. She felt frozen in time, the words repeating over and over until she felt as if she were going mad. *Dead on impact.* If she ran home right now, he would be there, waiting for her to play piano while he drank his evening brandy. No, he was dead. He was dead in the road, like some animal.

Then she was sobbing. Body wracking sobs and terrible cries of pain that did not even sound as if they came from her. Aunt Ebba gathered her up, pulling Amelia's head onto her lap and stroking her hair, but her fingers shook and caught as she too cried. Her father was gone. She would never see him again.

AMELIA'S THINGS WERE PACKED. The carriage waited outside the door, but still she could not bring herself to get up from her piano. It would be too real then. If she left here, her father would truly be gone. Foolish. He was dead. He was gone. She bit back the tears because she had learned if she allowed one out, many more would follow until she felt empty, and exhausted. There was nothing left to do but leave.

At last, when she knew she could delay it no longer, she went down to the door and out into the carriage. It started off and she leaned her head against the wall, praying for sleep. The journey to her family's country home would take the better part of a day, and she had nothing to entertain her but her own thoughts. Aunt Ebba promised to come and visit as soon as she could, but for now Amelia was alone. She had not even told Patience what had happened, and she dreaded the girl showing up at the townhouse and finding it empty.

Not one week after her father's death had letters begun to arrive. Most were condolences, but one was from her Uncle Declan, the man who had inherited the title of Duke of Ely. She had never met the man; Father had hated him.

It was a terse note, stating that he would come to explain "how things would be from now on" in regards to her lifestyle. Amelia could imagine all manner of things he might demand from her a frugal allowance, a banishment to a distant relative, but she was determined not to let it unnerve her. She was Lady Amelia Atherton, tough as a diamond.

Aunt Ebba had said nothing about it, other than that they would discuss it when she came to visit. In the meantime, she cautioned, do not spend more than you must to get by.

Amelia swallowed hard past the lump in her throat, putting such thoughts from her mind and tried once again to sleep but the jolting carriage made it impossible. It was a long and unpleasant ride.

WHEN SHE FINALLY ARRIVED HOME, the home she had grown up in, she could almost pretend her father was there. It smelled of him, of his cigar smoke and his cologne. It felt like an embrace. She spent the first day just sitting in his chair. The next day, she began sorting which things in her wardrobe could be repurposed for mourning attire. The small group of staff left at the house gave her space, for the most part, She refused all meals, keeping to herself and the rooms upstairs.

On the sixth day since her arrival home she went downstairs to the parlor and uncovered the piano, pulling off the sheet that had protected it from harm in her absence. She would not think at all of the future. She would not think of her father's death or her Uncle Declan looming in the not far distance. She would not think of how her life would change. There would be only this moment, suspended in time.

The first chord she played was awkward, not quite perfect, but she played it again, and again, until it was exactly what she wanted, *fortissimo*, a storm, a storm at sea. Tears welled in her eyes and grief constricted her heart, but all she felt seemed to flow from her fingers as she played: her passion released to the world. If she closed her eyes she could imagine her father there, in the chair across from her, tapping his foot in time with her music.

Part 2

Hidden Pages

6

The little fishing punt rocked side to side, unforgiving of even the smallest movement as it meandered idly down the river. It could not have gone any slower if Samuel Beresford had thrown down an anchor. Samuel shuffled restlessly.

"The point is to move slowly, Samuel, you needn't look so cross about it," said his brother, Percival.

Lord Percival Beresford had a fishing pole in hand and made a lazy cast, the hook landing not more than ten feet off the side of the boat. If you did not mind sullying the word by applying it the flat-bottomed craft Samuel had, for some idiotic reason, agreed to spend the day in.

"We are here for a day of idle recreation, so that I might take in the fresh air and thus aid my convalescence." Percival continued. "You did write mother?"

"I did," Samuel said. "Just as you said, but by the time I sent the letter, the doctor said you would recover. I only told her you weren't well and that that we had retired to the country at Stanherd Residence. I did not see any benefit to telling her the seriousness of the situation. If I done so she would have descended upon us in a heartbeat, with at least three doctors and her entire retinue from Bath."

"Very good," Percival replied. "I would not want to spoil her holiday."

Samuel just shook his head. Percy took decorum beyond the bounds of reason. He could be dying and would endeavor not to inconvenience anyone.

"It is very pleasant out here, is it not?" Percy asked.

"I think you are trying to torture me. You said we could take a boat out," said Samuel, kicking at one of the treads. "This is not a boat. This is a cabinet someone has flipped on its side and shoved out into the water. Then they give you a pole and say, here, push it along and have fun."

Samuel was being unfair. He was in fact grateful for the excuse to get out of the house, which had become more claustrophobic by the day. The reproachful quack of ducks as the punt passed their nests reminded Samuel of his father's constant harassments and he wanted to tell the ducks, and his father, that he would be gone before they knew it, so not to bother getting in a fuss...only his brother needed him. No matter that Percival would never admit it.

"Is this not what it is like to be in the Navy, then? It is rather how I imagined it, the water beneath you, the blue sky above, not a worry in the world." Percival was trying, unsuccessfully, to hide a smile. Samuel let him have it. If he was feeling well enough to tease, it meant he was at last on the mend.

The illness had come on Percival suddenly and violently at a ball in London. He had become quite ill, sweating and complaining of a burning in his mouth and stomach pain. He had originally blamed the ailment on a bad lamprey and didn't want to embarrass his host, the brothers had quietly quit the party and returned home.

Samuel had seen seaman sick from eating bad fish, and the best method of recovery was to rid oneself of the offending item, but once purged, Percy did not get well. The doctor had shaken his head and said that perhaps it was as they first thought a bad lamprey eel or a mushroom, but if so, he should get better.

Only Samuel wondered, why did no one else get sick? It pointed to a more sinister intention and a deliberate one. Days in bed had left Percy thinner than ever, almost gaunt, an unhealthy pallor marred his skin and he could barely eat without upset.

"We are on the water, and yes, there is a sky above us, but the similarities end there," Samuel groused.

As a commander in the Royal Navy he was rather used to a true ship. Samuel rose, legs bending to ride the motion of the boat, and used the pole to send them off again. Percival drew in his fishing line, empty. He had not had so much as a bite all day.

"Are you baiting the line, or just throwing it out?" Samuel asked. "I see a fish now, and look, there is one there. They are all around us Percival, how have you not caught a thing?"

"I should like to see you try," said Percy, tossing the fishing rod at Samuel.

Samuel caught it and knelt down to rebait the hook. He plucked one worm from their bucket of purchased bait and then cast the line out as far as it would go, well beyond the shadow of the punt. Though he had never fished before, having neither the leisure time nor the inclination, he had a fair understanding of the mechanics.

"There. Now it is only a matter of time," said Samuel. He sat down on one of the treads, gave the rod a twitch, and waited.

Percival leaned back against the till, arms behind his head, and puffed out a breath. "We shall see about that."

"Why are we out here, anyway? Not that I am complaining. I enjoy your company, but," Samuel gestured around with one hand, keeping the fishing rod steady with his knees. "This does not seem like your sort of activity. Are you so sick of Father?"

"No, but you are," said Percival. His eyes were closed and the puffs of his breath misted in the spring air. "I could see you were about to pull the cutlass off the wall at breakfast and run him through with it. I thought I was doing a public service by separating you two."

It was not unpleasantly cold, but brisk enough that Samuel had packed a blanket for Percy without his brother's knowledge. If he grew more ill because of this venture on Samuel's behalf, he would never forgive himself.

"Are you warm enough? There is a blanket in the basket. Go on and put it on, or I will never hear the end of it when we get home and you look the worse for wear," Samuel said, giving the line another shake.

Percy muttered something under his breath and yanked the blanket from the basket, wrapping it around himself before slumping back down against the till. He pulled it up to his chin and glared sulkily over it.

"Better?" he asked.

Samuel nodded. "He does not want me home, Percy. You know it as well as I do. If I had not joined the Royal Navy, Father would have found somewhere else to send me. He never wanted a second son. Hell, I think he would have been happier if I had been a girl, then at least he could have married me off and I would have become someone else's problem."

Percival was quiet for some time, until Samuel thought he had fallen asleep.

"He is proud of you," Percival said at last. "But I think he does not know how to deal with your moods. Not many people do."

"My moods?" Samuel frowned at the end of the line. He could see a fish swimming not ten inches from where the hook sat, baited with a tasty looking worm, but the damn thing swam on by. "I do not have moods."

"Right. Any luck with that fishing rod? Will there be fresh pike for dinner?" Percival pulled the blanket up to his nose, but not before Samuel caught the self-satisfied smile on his brother's face.

Instead of replying, Samuel reeled in the line, set the fishing rod down on the floor of the punt, and poled them to another section of the river. The grassy banks rippled in the breeze, undulating like a curtain. Almost he could smell salt and sea. He closed his eyes and took a deep breath, imagining the whisper of reeds was the sound of the ocean.

"Want another go?" Samuel asked, offering the rod to Percival.

He shook his head. "No, I think we can accept that fishing is not one of the Beresford brothers' innumerable talents."

"Speak for yourself," said Samuel. "I will catch a fish before we head home, mark my words."

"Joy, so we will be out here all day, then?"

"Are you ready to go in? Are you tired?" Samuel asked solicitously.

"No, no. I am fine."

This time Samuel baited the hook with two worms. If the fish were too stupid to take that deal, he did not want them anyway. He tossed the hook back into the water with a plunk and settled back against the side of the boat.

"I do not know how Father does not bother you, what with his constant nagging that you find a suitable wife. Are you certain you do not want to join the Royal Navy as well? I could put in a good word for you on the *Amelia*, have you off deck-scrubbing duty in no more than three months," said Samuel.

The mental image of his sizable brother scrubbing the deck beside the scrawny green boys normally given that role was quite entertaining.

"Tempting," said Percival. "I will think about it. But Father just wants to ensure the continuation of the line and the title Earl of Blackburn, as all noble fathers do. I think he worries that I am not truly searching for a wife, that I will turn out to be like you: Unmoved by anything but a well-turned schooner."

"That is not true," Samuel argued. He gave the fishing rod an irritated jerk. "But I have goals, brother, and having a wife and a child would only slow me down, hold me back. Maybe one day, when I have achieved what I want to achieve, I will consider it."

Percival grimaced. He was pale again.

"We should turn back and head home," said Samuel, but Percy held up a hand to stop him.

"Please do not. I am enjoying myself and am doing the same thing I would be doing at home, lying down, under a warm blanket, accomplishing absolutely nothing productive. What do you hope to achieve, Samuel? What true goals do you have?"

Samuel kept one eye on Percival, trying to appraise the situation without his brother calling him out, the other eye on his hopeful hook.

"I want to be a captain," said Samuel. He had wanted that since he was five-years-old and his father had given him a model ship. "To make my own fortune, my own life."

He still had that model ship, though one of its masts had been broken and the sails, darkened with age, were now a dingy shade of light tan.

"Why stop there? Why not Commodore Beresford? Or Admiral?" Percival was teasing him, he knew, but Samuel did not believe his dreams were out of reach if he remained focused.

"Laugh all you want, Percival, but I will be a captain

one day," said Samuel, letting a little of his annoyance show in his voice.

"I am not doubting you," said Percival, before breaking into another bout of coughing. "I hope you will, Samuel. I know you will. Not even the Lady Amelia Atherton could distract you."

The beautiful Lady Amelia Atherton had distracted a majority of the available gentlemen at the last ball he had frequented. He had wrested her from her pompous suitors and danced with her at that ball before Percival had fallen afoul of some enemy. He remembered how she felt in his arms and the faint scent of her perfume.

"Oh, she distracted me." Samuel mumbled under his breath

For all her bravado, she was still soft and impecunious, like any woman. Only she was not like any woman. Samuel sighed. He was not looking for a wife, and Lady Amelia was not the sort of woman for a dalliance.

"What was that? I could not quite hear you," said Percy. The coughing fit had brought a dangerous flush to his cheeks. It was time to head home, whether he wished to or no.

"I did not say a word," said Samuel. A sudden tug at the end of the line brought him to attention. He gave the pole a quick backward snap. "Percy, I think I have got something!"

Percy clambered to his feet, wobbling from the weakness or his lack of sea legs. "Liar. You just do not want to tell me what you said."

But he lurched his way over to Samuel and peered

over the boat's low wooden side. Samuel leaned back, fighting to pull in the fish.

"It must be a big one to put up such a fight," said Percy.

The water churned. With one final, mighty pull, Samuel yanked a carp the size of his forearm out of the river. It flopped onto the floor of the boat, tan and green scales glinting in the sunlight. Both men looked down at it in shock, and then smiled at each other.

"What do we do with it now?" Samuel asked.

Percy shrugged. "You are the great naval commander. You tell me."

"I feel rather bad now, seeing it flop about like that," said Samuel, kneeling down beside the struggling fish. "Shall we throw it back?"

"I think so," said Percy, but he stepped back with squeamish look on his face.

"Up to me then, I see." Samuel grasped the fish with one hand to hold it still and twisted the hook free with the other. Then, scooping it up with both hands he lowered it into the water. The carp wiggled off, disappearing into the murky depths with a few flicks of its powerful tail.

Samuel brushed his hands off on his trousers and stood, freeing the pole from its rest.

"Good thing you will be an Earl one day," said Samuel, getting the punt moving. "No hope for you as a fisherman."

Percival wrapped himself in his blanket and slumped down on one of the treads. "You are no better. If they ever run out of food on your precious *Amelia*, you would starve in a sea full of fish. You wanted to keep him as a pet, I saw it in your eyes."

"I just felt bad for the thing. Ripped out of the water and forced onto dry land. I felt a kinship with the creature, you might say," said Samuel.

"I am beginning to see Father's side," said Percival.

"If I dump you here in the river and you drown, do I get to be Earl? Why, I believe I do!"

Percy snickered. "You would rather drown with me than have that for your fate."

"Too true." Samuel replied and poled them back to shore at double time.

7

*L*ady Amelia Atherton paced nervously. She did not wish to play hostess to her Uncle Declan. He was her late father's younger brother and the new Duke of Ely, but the pain of losing her father was too new. Her father was the duke, not her uncle...only her father was gone. Her Uncle Declan, never her father's favorite relative seemed more like a vulture than a welcome guest. She knew her life now depended upon him, and she did not relish the change. The taste of the title, and the need to call him, Your Grace, felt sour in her mouth. She reminded herself she must be civil, even cordial, but she could not bring herself to do so.

When the time came, the new duke seemed as glad to be quit of her as she was of him. He arrived, demanded a meal at the odd hour of three o'clock, then left immediately after. During the hurried luncheon, he laid out his terms. She was to marry as soon as possible.

"Marry?" she said, thinking she was in mourning. Her

dear, patient, ever-present father was dead. The pain struck her again.

"Yes. Marry," the duke continued, telling her the allowance allotted to her.

It was a meager sum, so minute Amelia had asked him to clarify three times that it was the amount he had indeed intended. A dowry would be provided, as inadequate as the allowance. He had made her a pauper with only a word.

"For the time being," he said, "until the trouble of your father's debts has been attended to...

"Pardon," she said, drawing herself out of her moroseness and finding some of her nerve. "Debts? To whom? My father was a duke."

"Be silent. This is not a woman's business. You will stay here in the country and not stir up trouble until I sort out this mess." He gave her a hard stare, but no explanation. "It is seemly that you retire from Town in your grief."

She didn't argue, because her grief was sharp and she couldn't imagine ever dancing again anyway. She thought in that moment that the country would be soothing.

As abruptly as the duke had arrived, he left. Amelia had sat, with her food untouched, in a sort of shock for an hour after he had gone. She realized that although she had curtseyed and gave the bare minimum of courtesy she had not once called him 'Your Grace.'

Then she cried. She did not know what she was crying for, the grief of her father's death or the death of her life or both. It did not matter. She felt hollow, burnt out at the end of it. One of the maids had brought her a cup of tea and a tray of biscuits, but Amelia did not recognize her: A new member of the staff probably replaced by her uncle. All she had to look forward to was Aunt Ebba's visit, and she did not know when that was to happen.

She was to find a husband, while in mourning, with no funds to purchase new clothes nor even a respectable dowry to offer. Her uncle had made her task, one she did not wish to do anyway, that much more difficult. The scandal of her father's apparent debts would break out in London, whatever her uncle's efforts, and no man would want her. Debts? She thought. To whom? This seemed all too strange. Her father had not been upset by monetary problems. No, he feared for his person, not his finances....and now he was dead. She shivered.

Was it possible that somehow what he feared came to pass? Was it possible that he was truly indebted? Was that the reason for the carriage accident, or was it even an accident? No, she told herself. She was close with her father; even though she was a woman, she was his daughter. He would have told her to curb her spending if there were money problems. He would have told her. And now, because of his supposed debt, no matter neither how beautiful nor how desired Amelia had been just weeks ago, she would be untouchable.

Even if her uncle had not cloistered her here in the country, she would not have gone back to London. Propriety forbad her from attending any of the larger events just now, and she had no desire to further dishonor her father's memory.

Oh, she could just imagine Charity's gloating if she

did return. How she would relish seeing Lady Amelia brought low.

AMELIA WAS out in the garden on a walk when Aunt Ebba arrived. She had never been inclined toward the activity before; it only dirtied the hem of your dress, but she could not bear to be in the empty house for hours at a time. It echoed every footstep back at her, as if to mock her aloneness, besides dirt did not show so badly on black. Both she and her father spent a large portion of their time in London; the garden was in a sad state, overgrown and clearly untended, brambles and vines running over onto the stone path and trying to latch on to her ankle as she passed. If she had any talent or idea of what to do with plants, she would have tended them just to keep herself busy, but she had to settle for nudging them back behind the decorative garden wall with her slippered foot.

Aunt Ebba was waiting on the terrace, perched on the edge of her seat with a dainty cup of tea in her black gloved hand. She wore a large bonnet also draped in black gauze crepe; ever elegant even in her mourning garb. Amelia became acutely aware of her besmirched hem, and her slippers in no less of a state.

"Are you going wild out here in the country, my dear thing?" Aunt Ebba asked, with a pointed glance toward the sullied items. "Next time I visit, will I find you scurrying about on all fours and howling at the moon?"

"Hardly," said Amelia, raising her skirts to climb the

steps to the terrace. She lowered herself into the chair across from Aunt Ebba and poured herself a cup of tea. "I feel as though I am losing my mind here, Auntie. I never minded it before, though of course I preferred London, but now I feel so... alone. Alone with my thoughts, and I know none of the servants, thanks to Uncle Declan."

"He is a right piece of work, is he not? Your father and I spared you from having to deal with him as long as we were able. But there is nothing more I can do. He is the duke and you are here at his pleasure. If he wished to, he could remove you from this house as well, though he would be considered a rude and awful man by Society, I do not think it would stop him. So behave yourself, and give him no reason to think of you," Aunt Ebba said, and though she was primly sipping from her teacup there was intensity to her gaze that made her words sink like stones to the bottom of Amelia's stomach.

Uncle Declan was every bit as frightening as he seemed. If she were removed from the estate, there would be nowhere to go.

"I am always well-behaved," Amelia said, stung. "I have never been anything but the perfect gentlewoman, poised and witty and charming. And yet, here I am, banished with none of my friends and no hope of a suitor."

Amelia raised her eyes to the sky, fighting against the threatening tears. This place was clearly unhinging her, making her prone to the hysterics she had mocked in her London friends; Lady Patience and Lady Charity. Every emotion seemed a hair's breadth from bubbling over at the slightest provocation. Foolishness. She blinked back the tears.

"That is precisely what I have come to discuss with you. A suitor," said Aunt Ebba. She set her tea cup down on the saucer and clasped her hands on the table. "You must find a husband, Amelia, and the sooner the better."

They were the words she had expected, but knowing they were coming did not make them any easier to digest. Dread settled over her, a hot blanket despite the brisk spring weather.

"I know. That is what I had been doing in London, was it not? Attending balls and parties and—"

"No," Aunt Ebba cut in. "You have been playing, enjoying yourself, but not hunting for a husband. I did not object to your behaviors at the time. You were in no need to hurry into a marriage and a prize like you deserved to take her pick of the litter. But that leisure time is over, Amelia. Now the clock ticks down, and every second wasted lowers your chances."

Amelia dug her nails into the palm of her hand. She would not cry. What would crying do? Accomplish nothing.

"So I am a duke's niece instead of a duke's daughter. I am still Lady Amelia Atherton, and I believe it will not be such a great matter to find a husband," said Amelia.

The singing of the birds, the scent of the wild flowers, the sunshine, rubbed discordantly against Amelia's mood. It should be raining, or grey at least. Unbidden, the tune of a melancholy piece played in her mind. Better.

"I am afraid, you are tarnished by your father's

scandal, even if it is not so. I do not doubt that there will still be men who wish to marry you, who would be overjoyed to do so, but it will not be the same easy time of it you had before. And I know, Amelia that you never wished to marry. Your reluctance to do so showed through in your behaviors. That must change now."

"Of course I wished to marry, as every girl does," Amelia protested automatically, but Aunt Ebba's raised brow silenced any further arguments.

Aunt Ebba reached across the table and took Amelia's hand. Her face softened.

"I know you are frightened by what happened to your mother. I do not blame you for that, but you cannot let that fear control you, nor stop you from doing the things you must. She was a frail woman, often sickly, you are in the prime of health," said Aunt Ebba. "You will not die in childbirth."

The words were as much a slap in the face as they had been from Patience. Having one's fears laid out on the table was never a comfortable thing, especially when one believed them to be well hidden.

Amelia lifted her chin. "Very well. I am, however, banished to the country and have been given a meager allowance. I am hardly in the best position to be accepting visits from suitors. On top of that, I have no chaperone to make such visits acceptable."

"We will sort that out," Aunt Ebba said, releasing Amelia's hand and leaning back in her chair. "First things first, finding a suitor. Are there any men who have caught your eye? I could discreetly look into their interest when I am back in London."

"I will have to think about it," said Amelia. She would not inquire about Commander Samuel Beresford. He was a curiosity; she had danced with at the last ball she attended. Nothing more. "I will write to you, Auntie"

Aunt Ebba rose from her seat. "Very well, but do not dally."

They embraced and then Aunt Ebba was gone, leaving Amelia alone again. She watched the carriage fade into the distance, then turned and went into the house.

"Draw a bath for me, please," Amelia said to the maid. She needed a long hot soak and time to think. Find a husband, as if it were the easiest thing in the world. Oh, why could she not be like Patience and fall for the first man that smiled at her? If she were in love, marriage would not seem such a daunting thing. But Amelia had never felt that particular rush.

AMELIA SUNK into the bath to her chin, watching the steam curl up from the surface of the water. Father was gone now, and she had only herself. It would be enough. Find a husband, because it was the only way to ensure her happiness. She *would* do it, and she would do it quickly, before her uncle ruined her life. She waved the maid away and bathed herself with the bergamot-scented soap, scrubbing until the plan came together. There was no need for bright clothes, she was pretty enough to ensnare a man without ornamentation, and she would not settle, just because she was going through a troubled time. She was still Lady Amelia Atherton and she would get what she wanted, just as she always had.

She wrapped herself in a dressing gown and went to her desk, trailing water on the floor. The first note she crumpled and threw behind her. It was the third attempt that pleased her, and she rang for a maid to take it to be delivered at once. Her uncle would provide her with answers. Amelia deserved to know the depth of the scandal that had brought her father down, to do otherwise would be to go into battle unprepared. She also demanded he allow her to entertain suitors at the house, promising him it would take her far less time to find a husband if she did not have to run back and forth to London, unless he wished to give her use of the townhouse. That idea would be shot down, of course, he had been adamant about keeping her in the country. Though her blood was heated, she wrote dispassionately and persuasively, trying to capture her father's coolheaded manner that had served him so well. Oh Father, what did you do?

Every man had secrets, a private life. Amelia did not expect her father to have revealed all the sides of himself to her, but that she had had no inkling of any financial trouble whatsoever now made her fear the worst. Had he been involved in betting, or opium, or some black market trade? It was impossible to reconcile that picture of her father with the one she knew and treasured. Whatever had happened, she was positive it had not been his fault.

That evening, after dinner, Amelia did something she had never done before. She went upstairs and into her father's study. The room had always been off limits to her, a place for her father to retreat to and not be disturbed, and she had never questioned it before now. Now, he was gone, and there was nothing to stop her from going in there. Still, a thrill of nerves shot through her when she stepped inside for the first time. She had seen it only through a cracked door before, a glimpse stolen when her father was entering or leaving. The scent of him hung here, and she could almost believe he was still alive. It gave her a start. She took a breath and looked around the office.

It had two windows, and the curtains were drawn over them. Amelia lifted her candle higher and edged into the room. At the center of the room was a desk, still covered in papers as if her father had just stepped out for a minute, and might return. The walls were lined with bookshelves.

"He would not have minded," she told the empty room, as if it were judging her.

She hurried over to his desk before she could lose her nerve. She lit the tapers and set the candlestick down upon the desk. There was so much to go through, stacks and stacks of papers and leather-bound binders of ledgers. After an hour of searching through them and finding nothing out of the ordinary, she began to feel foolish and invasive, guilty that she had ever doubted her father. Then, when she went to slide one of the desk drawers closed, she felt something beneath her fingers on the side of the drawer. She pressed it, and heard a click. Out of the side of the regular drawer, a smaller drawer slid open. At first, she just stared at it. Her heart beat loudly in the silence of the room, an unsteady thumping she could feel in her ears.

"What is this, father? What were you hiding?"

She pulled the candlestick closer. The drawer contained only a few pieces of paper and a book. It may have once been cream-colored, but time and dust had turned it brown. Amelia felt, rather than saw, the embossed markings on the cover and held it up beside the light of the flame. A strange symbol was set into the surface, half of a circle struck through by two knife-like lines. If she had not touched it, she would never have known it was there. But what did it mean? And why was it hidden in a secret drawer, in a room no one but her father was allowed to enter?

A noise outside the door made Amelia bolt to her feet, heart pounding. She felt as guilty as a child caught sticking her finger into a fresh-baked pie. One of the servants banking the coals for the night, nothing more, she knew, but still she could not convince herself to calm down. Amelia gathered the papers hastily and snugging the book beneath her arm and her candle held in her free hand she left the room, pulling the door shut silently behind her.

The hallway was empty. Had she imagined the sound, just the product of a guilty conscience? She went straight to her bedroom and shut herself inside, tossing the contraband onto her bed. Setting the candle on the bedside table, she coaxed the fire in her room back to life then sat down beside the book. It would be a long night. She intended to read the thing cover to cover, only it was nonsensical. Each page had a list of words on it, words that were of no particular sensibility; words that did not even seem to belong in the same book.

Father, she wondered, what were you doing? Did it get you killed? A chill ran through her. She could no longer believe the falsehood that he had simply died in a carriage accident. It made no sense, and with the addition of these strange books, she felt a shiver of apprehension. She must find out the truth, but to do that, she needed to be in London.

"How can you miss London?" Samuel asked Percival, glancing up from his chart. "One can hardly breathe from the fog, move from the crowds, or think from the noise. Out here at least there is room and the air smells of grass rather than, well, you know." He wrinkled his nose thinking of the smell of offal in the streets.

At times it was hard for Samuel to temper his language. A lifetime on a ship did not produce the gentle language, and the words he used so casually would shock his lordly brother to the tips of his toes.

"I suppose there is something about it that pleases me, the same way life at sea pleases you. You cannot think I would enjoy that life. Living on dried, salty meat and spending my days at the mercy of the weather. It gives me the grippe to think about," said Percival. He was lounging on a chaise. The excursion in the fishing punt had shaken him. Despite Percy's assurances that he felt fine Samuel could see the strain, and he had eaten little, only taken a bit of tea.

Samuel tapped a finger on the thick parchment of the navigational chart. "This right here is a life of adventure, of opportunity. I do not need Father's approval or money. You will see. I only need a bit of luck and daring." said Samuel. "I only need a chance."

"You only need war," said Percival, "Although I suppose those happen often enough."

"I will make my own fortune. Once I am a captain, of course." Though the destruction of ships in the war did not make that future look promising. There were a number of commanders sent home on half salary and others on larger ships. Looking at an extended time under a captain instead of being given their own command; this was why Samuel was so determined to make captain himself.

Samuel looked back down at the chart. In his gut, he knew he would be a successful captain; all he needed was the opportunity.

"And if a storm comes along and sinks your ship, what good will a fortune do for you then? Gold sinks, my dear brother. Right to the bottom of the sea," said Percival, peering at Samuel through blurry eyes. "For that matter, a cannonball in the right spot could take you down just as easily. Will gold block a cannon shot? I do not think it will."

"It almost sounds as if you worry about me," said Samuel, with a grin.

But Percival was sober-faced as he replied in a soft voice, "I do, Sam, I do. Every day that you are gone I pray for your safety, but not for your return. I know that you are happier out there, that you belong out there, and so I pray for you to be the best damn commander the Royal Navy has ever seen."

"Language, Percival," said Samuel, but he was laughing. "What if Father were to hear you?"

"From London? That would be a feat," said Percy, weakly.

Percival was still thin but visibly healthier from when they had first retired to Stanherd Residence. At present Percival could only stomach the lighter fare of soups and porridge that the doctor had recommended. He seemed to be improving, but would revert back to his sickened state if his digestion was taxed by anything more substantial.

Samuel rolled up the chart and slid it back into its leather case, setting it beside the others. His father's library had an extensive collection of geographical charts, though Samuel had never figured out why, as the earl had little interest in nautical affairs beyond what a gentleman was expected to know.

"Speaking of Father, now that we have escaped the clutches of our nanny, what sort of mischief shall we get up to out here?" Samuel flopped down beside Percival on the chaise, nudging him over his hip. "Carousing, pillaging—"

"Samuel—"

"Gambling, racing—"

"Sam!" Percival broke in, snorting with laughter. "You may get up to whatever sort of trouble you wish. I will not stop you, nor tattle to Father. But I do not think my health is up to any of those activities, nor my spirit."

"Very well," said Samuel with a sigh. "We will just

lounge about then, reading books and sipping tea like a gaggle of old widows. Shall I send for an embroidery hoop and silk thread? My cuffs could use a bit of sprucing."

Percival was not too weak to plant a well-aimed elbow in Samuel's ribs. "You are incorrigible." He said with a smile

8

The effects Amelia had stolen from her father's office had raised more questions than they had answered. The book was encrypted in some manner. While the words on the page were legible and understandable individually, they meant nothing as a whole. They were only lists of words, periodically broken up by that strange symbol. The pages which she had originally thought were letters were actually a recopying of the book itself.

There was only one letter. The page bore no signature, but a hastily drawn version of the symbol marked the at bottom. It was dated a week before they had gone to London for the Season and included a poem. Had her father been writing poems for a lady? Though it gave her a queer feeling to think of it, she could not begrudge him the comfort of a woman ...or would not have...Oh bother. She sniffed and wiped her eyes on her handkerchief.

However on closer inspection she realized the poem was not written in her father's hand. Why would he hide this? And more importantly, did the date mean that more poems were present at their townhouse, and if so, had her uncle found them? Did he know what they were? Though she had no reason to believe it, Amelia was positive that the bizarre collection had something to do with her father's debts, and perhaps even his death. While she read them by candlelight, a sense of unease had filled her; there was something wrong with the words, some disturbing meaning hidden behind them.

It had been almost dawn when she had tucked the book and papers beneath the mattress and climbed beneath the covers for a few restless hours of sleep. Her dreams were troubled. She briefly considered writing her Aunt Ebba and enclosing a rendition of the symbol. Aunt Ebba knew many things and if anyone were to know the meaning of it, it would be her. But something stayed her hand. Some impulse told her to keep it to herself, or risk... something. The puzzle was yet another frustration.

Amelia had not received a response from her uncle, and it had her quite on edge. She was dreading him showing up on the doorstep to respond in person, but was dreading even more so a lack of a response entirely. Perhaps she should write him again and ask about the symbol. He might have known about it, perhaps that unknown handwriting was his. Or would that annoy him and cause him to refuse to respond out of principle? It was the not knowing that was driving her mad.

On top of her frustration, she was growing terribly bored. Though she spent hours at her piano and the rest of the time in the garden, she was a social person and this lack of interaction with any humans apart from the servants was intolerable. She had grown desperate enough to attempt to strike up a conversation with a chamber maid, but the girl was either too dumb or too startled to make anything intelligible come out of her mouth and Amelia had given up at once.

She felt caged here in the country, but even caged animals in a menagerie had onlookers to break the boredom. She tried to pass the time gardening although she had no talent for it. She pruned some of the larger rosebushes herself, and gathered some blooms in to brighten the dining room, but it did not brighten her mood. The next week of rain added to her melancholy and even her piano could not cheer her. When the rain finally passed, it left a chill in the air.

A BRIGHT MORNING a few weeks later, found Amelia in the garden once again. She shivered and thought she should have brought a shawl. The sun meant the weather to be warm, but the morning still held a chill, or was the chill only in her mind? She wondered.

It was with tremendous relief, that she heard the sounds of a carriage pulling up the drive. She rose from the garden bench and went at once to see who it was. Perhaps Aunt Ebba had returned.

"Amelia!" Lady Patience cried, as she stepped out of the carriage and saw her friend on steps of the manse.

Amelia's heart ached with happiness. She had not

realized how much she had missed the red-headed girl, not until she had seen Patience there with all of her usual easy emotion on her face. Here was her true friend. With none of her usual poise, Amelia gathered up her hem and raced down the stairs, catching Patience in a hug.

"Oof," said Patience, into Amelia's shoulder. "Are you quite all right, Amelia? This is most unlike you."

Amelia forced a big breath of air into her lungs and straightened, releasing Patience. "I am not myself of late, I confess. I hope I did not alarm you."

Looping her pinky finger around Patience's, Amelia walked back up the stairs and into the house. A dowdy older woman, Patience's maid, Amelia guessed, followed behind while two other servants carried in Lady Patience's luggage.

"I hoped to stay for some time," said Patience, catching Amelia's surprise, "If you do not mind. I would have written but I was worried you would say no. Of course you still might, but I thought it less likely if I were already here."

She said this all in a rush, as if she had to get it out before she lost her nerve. There was a new boldness to her, a streak of spirit Amelia had not seen before.

"I would not have refused you in a letter," said Amelia, though she was not certain she was telling the truth. Her embarrassment and shame may have caused her to do just that. It was hard to be seen by those who had known you before, once you were shamed. "But, Patience, you must know. My uncle has cut me off. I have barely sixpence to scratch together."

"Do you think I would no longer be your friend because you find yourself on hard times? Shame, Amelia. I am not so shallow."

"I am happy that you are here, Patience, so very happy, and I hope that will you stay for as long as you wish. To be honest, I have been lonesome out here in the country."

"It is very quiet." Patience admitted

Amelia directed the servants to put Patience's belongings away in one of the guest bedrooms, and then instructed them to set out tea on the patio. It was a perfect day, shining sun, blue sky, and many flowers were blooming. Sitting there, with the delicate china cup in her hand and a sweet citrus cake on the table, Amelia could almost pretend that nothing untoward had happened; that she was still the same Lady Amelia Atherton that she was before her father had died. Then Patience spoke, and the illusion shattered.

"Do you wish to hear what people are saying?" Patience asked gently. A slice of glaze cake sat untouched on her plate, and her cheeks were pink from nerves.

Amelia considered. She pushed a stray strand of hair out of her face. "It is all slum; I am certain. People believe the silliest things, especially when it involves a member of the Peerage or their kin. They are so eager to see us brought low."

Patience busied herself with her cake, and took a sip of tea but she didn't speak. Patience waited and finally Amelia nodded. "Tell me."

"The most popular rumor is that your father was

involved in some illegal activity, and the shysters got the better of him. That he is or was..." said Patience softly, "fairly flush in the pocket, and the money was paid to protect his name...keep it clear of the activities. When he did not pay..." She trailed off. She did not meet Amelia's eyes.

"Someone was blackmailing my father! That's ridiculous. And he would never be involved in something illegal." A chill crawled up her back as she thought of the book of cyphers. That certainly hinted at something untoward. *No. Not Father.*

"And the second rumor is that he was bankrupted by your spending habits; that you ran up bills at every shop in London."

Amelia reddened. "That is ridiculous. Both of them are. Of course I shopped, but it was well within our means, I..."

Amelia trailed off. She did not know if that was true. Obviously, it had not been within their means, she realized now. But father had never told her...

"That's just a fudge, of course," Patience said. "Even you could not spend enough to bankrupt a duke."

"So you believe my father was a criminal?"

"No. Of course not."

"What else are they saying?" Amelia asked.

"That your father's death was not an accident, either that he killed himself or..."

"Killed himself? By carriage?" Amelia said aghast.

"Or that he was murdered by one of the people he owed money to. It is awful, Amelia, the things they say. No one believes them," Patience insisted.

But Amelia knew she was wrong. There were many people who believed rumors; not those who loved her father, but there were always people willing to believe the worst. Amelia raised a brow. "No one? Not even Charity?"

"Well, perhaps Charity. She was always jealous of you, you know."

That Charity had nothing to be jealous of now, went unspoken between them.

"I do not know what is true, Patience," said Amelia, with a hitch in her voice. "The rumors could be true. Or something worse could be. There is this..." She hesitated. Should she tell Patience about the book? She shook her head. "My uncle has not told me anything, though I have written to him. It makes me fear the worst."

"I have heard he is a cold man," said Patience. She sipped her tea.

Amelia nodded. "He is nothing like father. I can see why they did not get along." Her voice softened to a whisper. "I do not think he wants me here."

"But what will you do, Amelia?" Patience asked. Her eyes were watery and Amelia felt herself tearing up in response. What was wrong with her?

"I will do as my Aunt Ebba has recommended and find a husband as soon as possible. It is the only way to get out from under my uncle's thumb and to prove that this disaster has not ruined me." Each time she thought of her plan, it strengthened her. "And I will find out what happened to my father, whether or not my uncle will tell me."

Patience was shocked, though Amelia could not imagine why, when it was obvious that there were no other options left to her. "A husband? But I thought you did not wish to be married."

"What I wish is no longer important, Patience, what I need is. And I need to be married, so I will be."

"But is there a man you have in mind?" Patience asked. "I have never seen you take a particular interest in one. Oh, well, except for that Navy man at the ball."

Amelia paused with the fork lifted as she remembered dancing with the handsome Commander Samuel Beresford, his awkward steps and witty repartee. He had been so brash, telling Lord Cornishe that he was boring her. Lord Cornishe *was* boring her, but it was so delightfully rude for the Commander to say so. And so she had danced with him. It was just a lark. She had thought it just a game at the time. After all, Samuel Beresford was below her, a second son, with no great inheritance or title. She was a duke's daughter, but now...

For just a moment she thought of his commanding attitude pitted against her uncle. He would get answers about her father's death of that she was sure.

Amelia frowned and dug her fork into the cake, wrenching a bite free. "I did not take a particular interest in that Navy man," she said. "However, I do have some rather exciting news for you on that account." Amelia said brightly eager to turn the conversation away from herself and her father. Patience perked up.

"You do? Is it about the gentleman I saw at the ball? Oh Amelia, how did you have any time to spare for my troubles when you've had so many of your own? You are too good a friend."

Amelia inclined her head graciously. "You are in luck, because the man you shared smiles with is the eldest son of the Earl of Blackburn. His name is Percival Beresford."

Samuel Beresford's brother she added silently.

"Percival Beresford," Patience repeated, her lips curling into a smile. "What a wonderful name."

Struck by sudden inspiration, Amelia said, "What if we were to invite Lord Beresford here? I have been so bored; a little gathering would be just the thing. We shall think of some pretense for it. I will ask my Aunt Ebba to help. I know she will. She knows I am positively wilting here with nothing to do. What do you think?"

"Oh my, I do not know. It seems so sudden, and awfully forward," said Patience, bringing one hand up to her freckled chest.

"Nonsense. Men love forward. And he smiled at you, did he not? He is clearly interested," said Amelia. In truth, she did not have the slightest idea if the man was interested, but she was desperate for a distraction, and just the thought of it made her feel more herself.

"If you truly think so," said Patience, breathless.

"I do," said Amelia.

AMELIA COMPOSED a letter to Aunt Ebba and sent it off straight away. Four days later, they had a response. Patience and Amelia sat down on the sofa to read it, side by side, in front of a fire, as the spring weather had turned rainy and damp. Aunt Ebba was thrilled to hear that Amelia had a friend staying with her, she had been worried about her emotional state, and she would be happy to attend in a chaperone capacity for their little get together. However, and here Patience grabbed hold of Amelia's hand, she had news that Lord Beresford had taken ill after the last dance, and sequestered himself away at his country estate while his health recovered. She would write to him and inquire as to whether he was well enough for such an excursion.

"Oh goodness," said Patience, when Amelia had finished reading the letter aloud. "I cannot believe he is ill. How awful. We cannot have him over; the traveling could cause him to relapse, especially if this damp weather continues."

"You are being frantic, Patience," said Amelia. "It is probably nothing more than a mild sickness, you know how the end of winter brings those on, and Lord Beresford will be grateful to have something to lift his spirits. That will be you!"

"Are you certain?" Patience asked.

Amelia tried to resist sighing at Patience nervousness. "Yes, darling, I am certain."

Although Patience had done wonders for her own spirits, Amelia was far from certain of Lord Beresford's feelings, but now that she had a potential distraction at hand she refused to give it up. Amelia penned a brief response to her aunt thanking her.

That evening she played her work in progress, a song for the sea, on the piano trying to devise the next movement. It occurred to her that the piano now belonged to her uncle, and she became discouraged. She retired to her bedroom for the night. She did a bit of needlepoint and read for a while, but the tasks did nothing to relax her. In the end, she opened father's book again and read the lists of words trying to decide what they meant. She fell asleep with a poem in her lap.

9

*S*amuel Beresford took the letter from the footman and waved him away.

"That is for *Lord* Beresford, sir," said the footman, still standing there, eyeing the letter as if he meant to wrest it out of Samuel's hands. Samuel gave the footman a hard glare and tucked it beneath his jacket.

"And my elder brother is too ill to be reading his own correspondence, so I will take this to him straight away and read it aloud for him. Now go," said Samuel. He turned around before the footman could lodge another rude protest and went to find Percival. It was a good thing the man was not under his command, Samuel thought uncharitably. He pondered what he would do with him: sack him; beat him; throw him overboard. Samuel smiled at the thought, but he knew he was just anxious being on land so long. It was not the footman's fault.

Percy was, Samuel was pleased to see, sitting up in their father's office. There was a nearly empty cup of tea at his side and yet another half-eaten meal. Samuel surveyed the nearly whole fowl, crisp and spiced, but the soup and potatoes were picked over, which was more than he had seen Percy eat in weeks. Some color had returned to his face and he did not shake so.

"Why Percival, I do believe you have managed to swallow a whole cup of tea," he said with light rancor.

Percy scowled at him. "I ate the potato," he said. "And the soup."

"And you almost look like one of the living now, rather than a corpse dragged out of the river," said Samuel, lightly. He did not tell his brother that he had truly worried for his life just a few short weeks ago. "Oh well. I guess I shall not become Earl after all," Samuel said tossing himself into one of the armchairs beside the windows. "And I shall have to continue to look on your sullen face."

"Is that how you say you care about me? No wonder you must pay women for their company," said Percy. He did not glance up from the book he was reading. The cover was so worn Samuel could not make out the title. It almost looked like someone had fished it out of the bilges.

"Almost funny, brother, keep trying and I am sure you can find a sense of humor somewhere," said Samuel. "I have a letter for you."

"Hand it over, then," said Percival, holding out one hand.

"Nonsense. As I told the footman, you are too ill to be reading, so I shall it read it to you," said Samuel.

"One is never too sick for reading," Percy said as Samuel unfolded the letter and scanned it.

"Well? Are you going to read it out or just keep it to yourself? It is my letter, you know. Who is it from?" Percival asked, sliding a bookmark between the pages and shutting the book at last.

"You will not believe this brother, but it is from Lady Amelia Atherton," said Samuel.

Percy snorted. "I am sure it is. Give it to me, if you are just going to make up tall tales."

Samuel flung the letter over to his brother. "See for yourself."

Percy read it and then reread it, his brow growing more and more furrowed with every word. "Did you have something to do with this, Samuel?"

Samuel shook his head. He got up from his chair and prowled around the room, opening cabinets until he found the crystal bottle of brandy, which he took back with him to his armchair. "Do you know the woman she mentions? This 'friend you met at the ball'?" He asked as he poured.

"Perhaps... it could be the woman I passed, but what are the chances of that? She was so pretty," said Percival, smiling at the memory. "Riotous red hair," he said fondly. "But it could not be. How fortuitous, that we would find each other again, despite not having ever been introduced. It's almost as if it is fate's hand, reaching out to us. It would be too strange. Do you not think so, brother?"

As much as Samuel would have wanted to tell his brother to go and enjoy himself, he could not see his way clear to allowing it. He had horrible visions of his brother toppling from his horse. "You are too ill to be riding out there," said Samuel. "We will have to write back and tell her no; you will not be coming to visit."

"Nonsense," said Percy. He opened drawers in the desk until he found paper and ink, then set straight to writing. "I will accept the invitation, and tell them you will be joining me. That way you can make sure I do not strain myself."

Samuel almost coughed out his mouthful of brandy. "You will do no such thing. I do not want to spend another moment in Lady Amelia Atherton's company. If father found out that you travelled again after the doctor's strict orders that you do not exert yourself, he will be furious at me for allowing it. Besides, what about all the light foods the doctor ordered? Who will prepare them?"

"I am not a child," Percival complained. "I feel like all I eat is milk and porridge."

"And that is why you finished your quail," Samuel said gesturing to the nearly untouched bird on his plate.

Percival's face fell, and Samuel sighed. He wanted to help his brother get well, but healing his body, seemed to be at the expense of his heart. His foolish brother had already fallen for a girl he did not know, and now Samuel had no choice but to help him court her. He could not let his brother down.

"Very well then, invite them."

"Invite them," Percival said. "Here?"

"Why not? Tell them you are not up to travel. If they accept, fine, if not, you can go another time. That seems best, don't you think?" Samuel got up to look over Percival's shoulder as he wrote out the new reply. His brother's hand was not as crisp and eloquent as it was in good health, but it still was far more legible than it had been just a week ago. He had apparently been copying a poem...for his lady love, Samuel wondered.

Samuel glanced down at the book on the desk. Papers were scattered around beneath it, filled with unknown handwriting and some of Percival's. At this range, he could make out the details of the cover. The brown leather was embossed with a strange symbol, one Samuel had never seen before, a semicircle crosshatched by two sharp lines. Once he had seen it there, he spotted it twice more on the papers, written like a signature, at the bottom of the page.

"What is that?" he asked, pointing at the symbol.

Percy moved with a speed Samuel had not known he had, gathering up the papers in his arms, including the poem and flipping the book over, which Samuel now saw, was heavily water damaged. He dumped the bundle into a drawer and shut it again.

"Just ledgers. Boring things that father wanted me to look over," said Percival, not meeting Samuel's eye. He shifted nervously in his seat.

Samuel knew at once that Percy was lying to him. It was so rare a behavior from his brother that he could hardly believe it, and had no idea how to respond.

"I see," said Samuel. "Nothing I wish to get involved with."

Percival laughed a strained high sound. "No, certainly not. Will you post this for me, brother?"

Percival sealed the reply to Lady Amelia with hot wax and handed it to Samuel. Mutely, he took it, getting the distinct impression that he was being dismissed.

"Will all of those fit in here?" Patience asked, peering out of the carriage window at the train of servants. They were all weighed down by luggage, Aunt Ebba's luggage, and were attempting to stow it in the carriage. Patience and Amelia had brought two pieces each, but Aunt Ebba had at least ten to herself.

"I do not think so. Aunt Ebba will throw a fit if it does not, so that will be entertaining to see," said Amelia, settling herself back against the seat. Waiting for Aunt Ebba was an act of enormous patience. She took hours to get ready for anything, even for traveling, and the more fuss she could build up around it, the more pleased with herself she was.

Sure enough, Aunt Ebba stormed out of the front door a minute later and began berating the servants. Three of her luggage pieces had fit and the rest were sitting on the stone drive. Amelia turned from the scene and closed her eyes.

"She is on a tear," said Patience, rubbing her hands together nervously. "Should we do something? Offer to help?"

"The only way we could help is by giving up our seats so she may pack her things in here. Do you want to walk behind the carriage all the way to Beresford's estate? I do not. No, it will pass. She does not need half of the things she is bringing," said Amelia.

"What if we only brought one piece each? Then she could fit two more. Oh dear, she is rather cross now," said Patience. "I think I should go out there."

Amelia reached across to stop Patience from climbing out of the carriage. "You are liable to get your own head chewed off if you go out there. And nonsense, we need everything we packed because we are not prone to excess as she is."

Amelia could not leave behind a case because tucked in one of them, wrapped in a shift, was the book and the papers she had stolen from her father's office. She was not certain what had compelled her to bring them, only that she could not bear to leave them behind and risk one of the staff finding them when they cleaned her room.

Two of the servants ran back to the house with a suitcase in each hand. The carriage rocked and shook as the remaining servants attempted yet again to squeeze the remaining cases in.

"Good heavens," said Patience. "Is this what seasickness feels like?"

"You are just nervous about meeting Lord Beresford on proper footing. You will have to do more than smile at him today, though you look lovely," said Amelia.

Patience was outfitted for traveling in her new yellow dress with a moss green spencer jacket and a green bonnet bedecked with small yellow flowers. Amelia had purchased the bonnet for her as a gift before all the trouble started. Additionally tucked away in Patience luggage was a dinner dress in a deeper shade of emerald that set off her porcelain skin and flame-red hair. It was one of Amelia's and of a more daring cut than Patience had worn before, but Amelia had insisted, pleased that Patience could look stunning even if she could not. Amelia herself was still restricted to black crepes but that was all to the better since the attention would be focused on Patience alone. This was her friend's chance for a husband, and Amelia would not spoil it.

The carriage door swung open and Aunt Ebba in a long pelisse coat of black bombasine climbed inside, huffing. "The incompetence is astounding, truly astounding. I should have brought a second carriage, if I had only been thinking properly. Tuck your legs in girls, there you are."

A servant slid a suitcase on the floor between the seats; then stacked another on top of it.

"Really Aunt Ebba, is this necessary?" said Amelia, wedging herself into the corner so she might have some space. Patience was nearly in her lap. "We will only be there for a week. You have brought enough clothes to attend Court for a month."

Aunt Ebba sniffed. "In order to look one's best; one must have choices, even in mourning. Moreover, I thought we might share, but if you would rather not..."

"It is a wonderful idea to have brought so many options," said Amelia, forcing a smile to her face. She had been lusting after her aunt's wardrobe since she was old enough to walk.

"I thought so," said Aunt Ebba.

The carriage set off. Amelia felt sorry for the horses; they had probably never pulled such a heavy load before.

At least it was not a long journey, as the Beresford's country estate, Stanherd Residence, was only ten miles away. Crammed in as they were, however, ten miles might as well be one hundred. It was evening by the time the carriage slowed, and Amelia's body was protesting the tight quarters and the jarring of the carriage. She clambered out the moment it halted and sucked in the fresh air. Patience tumbled out after her.

"Is my bonnet disheveled? It cannot have survived that journey," said Patience, fretfully. She fussed with the flowers, making more a mess of them than they had been. Amelia swatted her hands away.

"Let me do it," she said, straightening the flowers and tugging a few curls loose to hang around the other girl's face. "Now stop worrying and smile. Do you not know that is your best feature?"

"Why are we dawdling out here? Come on, inside," said Aunt Ebba, shooing them both toward the house.

"Are you ready?" Amelia asked. She looked back at her luggage, which would be brought to her room by a servant shortly, but she did not like to have the book far from her for even that long.

Patience nodded, shooting Amelia a nervous grin. "I think so."

Looping their pinky fingers, Amelia and Patience marched up the steps.

"PERCIVAL, ARE YOU READY YET?" Samuel called from the other side of Percy's bedroom door. He rapped his knuckles against the wood for the third time. "Are you feeling ill again?"

Samuel glanced at his watch. The women would be at the house within the hour and he did not want to meet them alone. Did not want to meet them at all, in fact, but he would do what he could for Percy, as any good brother would.

"Yes," came Percival's reply.

"Yes you are ready, or yes you are feeling ill?" Samuel asked, rolling his eyes up to the ceiling. He had been dressed and ready two hours ago and had already broken into the brandy.

"Yes to both." The door opened and Samuel stepped back as Percival walked out. His brother's face was ashen, but his clothes cut a dashing figure and he did not look as if he had been ill for weeks. "I think this was a terrible idea. We should send them away."

"I am not the heir of an Earldom and even I know that would be unspeakably rude of us," said Samuel. He took Percival by the arm and steered him down the hall and down the staircase. "Just have a drink and perk up, you are about to meet your future wife! Or something like that."

"You are not very good at this, you know," said Percival.

Samuel poured them both two fingers of brandy. Percival accepted the glass but took a cautious sip as if the fine brandy was vinegar.

Samuel took a healthy swig from his own glass. "Oh, do slow down, Percy," he said. "I do not want you passing out before the ladies arrive. Three of them and one of me." He put on his best lecherous grin.

"You are a scoundrel, Sam," said Percy, shaking his head and putting the glass aside just as the call came from their butler.

Samuel straightened Percy's cravat and gave him an encouraging slap on the shoulder.

"Off we go then," said Samuel, pushing him toward the door. "Go and greet your guests, oh Lord Beresford."

"Did I forget to tell you? I poisoned your brandy," said Percival, as he walked to the door. Samuel supposed that he should be grateful Percival could joke about poisoning, but the words only made a shiver run down his spine, like someone walking over his grave. They had not found the person who done the deed or why. It gave Samuel no rest.

"Your threats would be far more convincing if I did not know how badly you need me here," said Samuel "These women would have you tongue-tied in moments, if I were to suffer an untimely demise."

In fact, when the door opened and the three women were showed inside, it was Samuel who could not find his voice. Lady Amelia Atherton stood in the doorway, framed by the sunset, and looking lovelier than he remembered. Samuel's heart did something it had never done before except in the midst of a battle; it skipped a beat.

10

——————

Side by side, the two brothers looked almost identical. Commander Samuel Beresford was a broader, more muscular, and Lord Percival Beresford was an inch or two taller. Lord Beresford had lost weight in his illness, but there was no mistaking the family resemblance. Once the brothers moved and talked, their mannerisms and demeanor could not have been more different. Amelia had seen a little of Samuel's character at the ball, his bravado and carelessness, but his elder brother was the opposite. Percival was gentle and almost anxious in his speaking, and he reminded her at once of Patience. If the shy pair did not spend the entire time getting in each other's way, they would be a splendid match. As it was, they could not make eye contact without blushing or breaking into nervous smiles, so there was much work to be done.

Amelia realized she was focusing on Lord Beresford and his greeting of Patience because she was trying to avoid thinking about Commander Beresford. She knew he was staring at her though, could feel the heat of his gaze, but she refused to acknowledge it. Did he harbor a mistaken belief that she felt something for him, just because of their brief interaction at the ball? She would need to correct that assumption straight away. If only she could manage to look at him, or better yet, say anything. The words seemed to die on her tongue. Patience must have rubbed off on her during the carriage ride because there was a traitorous flush on her cheeks whenever she dared to glance at the Commander.

Aunt Ebba, her earlier annoyances forgotten, was the only thing saving the room. She was warm and friendly, slipping into the role of chaperone with ease. Once all of their belongings had been taken upstairs, the three women followed them up to their guest rooms.

After a quick glance in her bedroom, Amelia met with Patience and the two girls huddled into Aunt Ebba's room.

"Is this your first outing?" Aunt Ebba said, as she smoothed the wrinkled creases of her dress. "You two are acting like nervous debutantes, afraid to step away from the wall. I thought this was your idea, Amelia, and I have never seen you anything but the perfect guest. Pray tell me what is the matter?"

Two maids knocked on the door, and Aunt Ebba bade them enter with their basins of scented water.

Aunt Ebba gave the perfumed basin of water over to Patience, gesturing that she should wash, and then turned back to the vanity and studied her own face. She wiped it with the damp cloth and then turned back to the girls.

"I am sorry, Auntie," said Amelia, digging for an excuse. She did not even know how to explain it herself. "I think I am still grieving Father, and it catches me off guard at the oddest times."

"Sit down, Patience," said Aunt Ebba, giving up the pouf at the vanity. "Well, I hope you will overcome Amelia and not leave dear Patience with the burden of socializing on her own. You must support her. Lord Beresford is a perfect match for her, and we must put our best feet forward to help her make it."

The maid silently straightened some of Patience's red curls, but her hair just would not smooth. Amelia almost felt sorry for the poor girl. Aunt Ebba brushed her away and repined some of Patience's curls herself. Then she began applying powder to Patience's face.

"Those are freckles, not blemishes," Patience protested, when Aunt Ebba, frowning went over them with the powder yet again.

Aunt Ebba stepped back to inspect her work, lips pursed. "An improvement, at least."

"She means you look beautiful, Patience" said Amelia, frowning at her aunt as she wiped sweat and dust of the journey from her own face and neck.

Patience did not look convinced.

With a jolt Amelia remembered the cypher book she had smuggled from home. It was not truly her home anymore at all anymore. The estate was Uncle Declan's, and although she doubted she would have much time to peruse the strange book here, she could not leave it behind. Not if the book might be of some help in discovering what her father was doing, especially if it contained some clue about his death.

"I will be back in a moment," she said, rushing off to her bedroom.

Thankfully, her luggage was sitting beside the bed, not yet unpacked. The maids must have started with Patience's or Aunt Ebba's things. She opened the latch of the larger trunk and retrieved the book from its hiding place in her shift. Then, she tucked it beneath the mattress, closed her luggage, and left the room. That had almost been a major mistake. Any servant unpacking her things would have been immediately suspicious of the way the book was packed; clearly intended to be hidden. Those were not questions she could afford, nor gossip she wished spread. Amelia chastised herself for her carelessness; it was most unlike her.

As she hurried from the room, she nearly collided with a maid coming to unpack her trunk and collect her dress for dinner. The slight girl reddened and curtseyed. "Your pardon, M'lady, I have just come to unpack. Is there something you needed?"

"I was just looking for...nothing. It doesn't matter," Amelia said.

"Did you have a preference for which dress you would like to wear for dinner?"

"Bring the dinner dress with the curved borders at the bottom."

"What was all of that about?" Aunt Ebba asked, when Amelia scurried back into her Aunt's room a minute later. She was standing behind Patience, fiddling with the poor girl's hair again. It looked painful, from the expression on Patience's face.

"I wanted to see if they had unpacked my tortoiseshell comb," Amelia lied, touching a hand to the top of her hair. "But they have not, and I did not want to search for it. Oh well, I will have to go unornamented into the fray."

"Hmm," said Aunt Ebba. She had finished with Patience, who now backed well away against the wall in case Aunt Ebba should decide to attack some other matter of her appearance. "I think I have something for your hair, but first, sit down Amelia. You could do with a little color in your cheeks and you have dark circles under your eyes."

"Surely not," Amelia said, bringing a hand to her face, but before she could protest further, Aunt Ebba steered her by the shoulders onto the pouf and set to work.

"I do not need any of that," Amelia said, trying to swat her aunt away. "I have never worn any powder before."

"You look tired," said Aunt Ebba, in a no-nonsense tone. "Trust me. Now sit still or it will take longer."

When Aunt Ebba had finished, Amelia had to agree there was a noticeable difference to the better. She had not realized how much the events of the past weeks had affected her, until the shadows below her eyes were covered and a little life was brought back to her cheeks with Aunt Ebba's pinching. Grief, worry, all of those things took a toll.

Amelia thanked her aunt just as maids came in with their dresses for dinner. Even in mourning Amelia felt she cut a figure. Her black silk dress, worn over a sarsnet slip, had two crescent shaped borders with tiny bows at the points. It was cut low and square around the bust and trimmed with a tucker of crepe and black bugle beads. Aunt Ebba was just as elegant in a gown made tight at the throat, with crepe ruff at the collar and a cap of black feathers. Though Patience was truly the light of the evening in the emerald green gown. It was a light tulle with puffed sleeves and hem; trimmed in white satin around the bust gathered with tiny green rosettes. Patience wore a necklace of glittering topaz with a matching haircomb and white satin gloves; while Amelia completed her ensemble with black kid gloves and a simple string of jet black pearls.

These reminded Aunt Ebba of the hair ornament she spoke of for Amelia and it was another ten minutes after they dressed for Aunt Ebba to find and place a black beaded band to her liking, in Amelia's hair. Then ten after that before she declared the three of them acceptable to go down for dinner. By that time, the brothers were probably wondering if they had fallen asleep, for it had taken well over an hour for the whole ordeal.

Indeed, the brothers were waiting in the parlor. Commander Samuel Beresford had a brandy glass in hand and Lord Percival Beresford was seated with a book. He rose when they entered. Samuel did not, though his gaze was fixed like the barrel of a gun on Amelia, shamelessly staring. She matched it, but he did not flinch back, nor look away. In fact, the man grinned at her with a twinkle in his eye. Grinned!

"I hope your rooms were acceptable," said Percival, with a warm smile he shared with all three women, but widened when looked at Lady Patience. "Dinner is ready, if I may escort you ladies to the dining room."

"Please do, Lord Beresford" said Aunt Ebba. She laid her hand on Percival's arm, and Amelia and Patience fell in behind them.

Commander Beresford still did not rise. Amelia raised her voice loud enough for him to hear, but aimed the question at Percival, "Will your brother not be joining us?"

"Oh he will, he will," said Percival, voice tight. "He just... likes to do things in his own time. And his own way. Younger brothers, you know. Or perhaps you do not. Do you have any siblings, Lady Amelia?"

He was babbling, a trait Amelia found quite annoying in a man but somehow, knowing it was due to Patience's nearby presence, became rather endearing.

"I do not," she replied. "I am an only child."

"Count yourself lucky," said Percival dryly.

"I did hear that," said Samuel, from not too far behind them.

The dining room was lit by candlelight, a grand crystal chandelier hung above the table and its four tiers danced with the orange flames. The covered trays of food had filled the room with savory scent that made Amelia's stomach rumble. She clasped her hand over it, embarrassed.

"A long journey, excuse me," she said. What part of her would rebel next? First her mind, then her complexion, and now her stomach! She was falling apart. A servant pulled out her chair and she sat down upon it before her body could find some new way to embarrass her.

Just as everyone else took their seats, Commander Beresford strode in. He did stride, not walk, nor glide. It was a purposeful movement, as if he had to be certain of each placement of his foot before deciding to take the step. Stopping by a servant, he handed off his empty brandy glass and, after sitting, picked up his wine glass straight away. Somehow, the alcohol did not seem to be affecting him, though any other man would have been glassy-eyed from the amount of brandy. Amelia sniffed primly and looked away.

"Will the Lord Blackburn be joining us?" Aunt Ebba asked Percival, interrupting the awkward tension that had built during the late entrance.

Lord Beresford shook his head, and gestured for the servants to begin the dinner service. He picked up his wine glass but did not sip from it, using it more, Amelia thought, as a way to keep his hands busy while he talked.

"I am afraid not. My father returned to London for the remainder of the season," he said. "Normally, I would have stayed in town with him, but I have only recently recovered from a ...an illness. Do not fret; the doctor promises me it is not catching."

"A good thing too," said Samuel. "If you had only seen him,—"

"Thank you, Samuel," Percival cut in.

Samuel tilted his glass toward Percival.

"Well, I am so happy that you have made a full recovery," said Patience, her voice unnaturally high. "The countryside truly is the best place for convalescence. I find it so refreshing, particularly in the spring time."

"Indeed. Though I confess, I am not accustomed to spending so much time out here and have found myself searching for things to do, though of course there are countless activities," Percival said.

"We did try fishing," said Samuel.

"And how did that fair?" asked Amelia, trying to imagine Commander Beresford sitting still long enough to catch anything. He was constantly moving, shifting, as if he could not get comfortable in his own skin. "As a Naval man, I would expect you could handle a fishing skiff with ease."

"Oh he handled the punt just fine," Percival replied. "It was the fishing itself that tripped him up."

"I beg your pardon," said Samuel, sitting his glass down on the table with a clunk. Luckily, it was empty. "I believe I caught a fish, which is far more than you managed."

"Well, that sounds like a successful fishing trip to me," said Patience, trying to calm the situation. Her freckles were standing out beneath the powder, a clear sign of her rising nerves. "If the whole goal is to a catch a fish?"

Samuel held a hand palm out toward Patience. "As the lady says. A successful fishing trip. For me. The one who caught the fish."

Percival snorted. "My dear brother neglects to mention that I was still convalescing at the time and, wrapped in a blanket, did not have the wherewithal to manage the rod."

"Is this becoming a common activity with the gentlemen your age?" Aunt Ebba asked.

"It is. A leisurely boat ride, an excuse to spend an entire day outside," said Percival.

"I would hardly call it a boat," Samuel said, under his breath. He had demolished his bowl of soup and was working on his glass of wine. "But I suppose beggars cannot be choosers."

They were interrupted by the clearing of the first course and the arrival of the second, a glazed pheasant stuffed with berries and vegetables. The footman carved the meat in paper thin slices, and served portions to each as they spoke.

"He waxes eloquent about his time at sea, but he is always very eager to eat a proper meal," said Percival. "So I do not believe it is the glamorous life that he insists it is. All adventure, all of the time, and no mention of seasickness nor the close quarters nor the need to survive on hardtack alone."

"You would not switch roles?" Patience asked. "No latent desire to walk in the other's shoes?"

Samuel and Percival replied in unison, "No!"

All three of the women laughed. Percival and Samuel both looked horrified at the idea of such a thing.

"I would be bored to death in two days," said Samuel, scoffing. "What does a lord do all day? Little. What does the heir of a lord do all day? Even less."

Percival shook his head with the look of a man who had had this argument many times before. "If you were forced to live my life, brother, you would not be bored, you would be overwhelmed. It is great responsibility, and we both know that is something you cannot abide—something or someone needing you."

"But that cannot be true," said Amelia. She shot a furtive glance at Commander Beresford, who was looking at her with an intense, dark gaze. "For at the ball we attended, you spoke of your desire to one day become a captain, and that is also a role that must involve a great deal of responsibility. Not only are the men beneath you dependent upon you, but the ship as well. If something were to go wrong, the ship were to sink or the men to fall victim to plague, it would be on your head, would it not?"

"Lud," Patience exclaimed. "Plague?" She shuddered. "Amelia, that is too awful to think about."

Commander Beresford leaned toward her. His leg brushed against hers beneath the table, she could feel the heat of him through his breeches, through her skirts. Amelia resisted the desire to pull away, knowing it would satisfy him to know he had affected her, so she looked him straight in the eye and refused to move. She was gratified to see his eyes widen in surprise, but a moment later his knowing smile was back.

"You are looking at it all wrong, as my brother always does," said Samuel. "All of the glory, all of the success! That is mine to claim as well, if I were a captain."

"I am sure you do your duty well," Aunt Ebba interjected placidly. "We are all grateful for our Royal Navy and their exploits and daring."

"Glory for your country? Glory for the Royal Navy? Or glory for one Commander Samuel Beresford?" Amelia asked, with an eyebrow raised. "Are not the navy and navy men, even captains duty bound to serve King and Country?"

"Do not censure me, Lady Amelia. As your good aunt points out, for whom but King and Country am I chasing down the privateers that run contraband to the French? Assisting that devil Napoleon and giving him succor. If not for our fine ships, we would find the blackguard at our border, dear lady, attempting to take England as he has thought to run over the continent."

"Oh dear," said Patience.

Samuel took a drink of wine. "I have brought many to the King's justice, or to a watery grave."

"Samuel, I expect this is not fit discourse for the ladies. My brother is ever the seaman. He forgets himself," Lord Beresford said.

"Of course," said Amelia. "I'm sure he is a fine officer who keeps us all safe. There is nothing wrong with being proud of one's accomplishments."

"Just so," Lord Beresford said.

Amelia took a small bite of her pheasant. She noticed that both Lord Beresford and Patience had hardly touched their food.

"Truly," Commander Beresford said. "I would not expect you to understand. Have you ever had anything to be so proud of? Something you can call your own?" Samuel asked, shaking his head as if to already dismiss her answer. "I did not think s—"

"Yes, as a matter of fact," Amelia broke in. "I play the piano, and I am most proud of my abilities."

"She is excellent," said Patience, her voice trembling.

She looked from Samuel to Amelia and back again. "Perhaps she would play for us after dinner?"

"Do you keep a piano?" Amelia asked, jolted from her rancor by the idea.

Aunt Ebba breathed a sigh of relief, which Amelia pretended not to hear.

"We do," said Percival. "It should even be in tune. Our mother plays."

"Is Lady Blackburn in London?" Aunt Ebba inquired.

"No," Percival said. "She is currently in Bath with her sister. She prefers the air there to London. Although I am surprised she did not travel back to chaperone when she heard we were to have guests."

"Oh, I did not tell her," Samuel said flippantly. "Anyway, the ladies lovely Aunt Ebba is here for that."

The rest of dinner passed with the usual sort of friendly talk, mainly between Lord Beresford and Aunt Ebba. Commander Beresford was sitting, sulking really, in silence apart from the occasional jab he snuck in toward his brother, and occasionally glancing at Amelia when he did not think she was looking. His leg had not moved away from hers. Patience, flustered by the near-argument between Amelia and the Commander, did not speak much, but every time Lord Beresford looked at her she broke into a smile.

After dinner, the group made their way to the piano room and took seats on the plush sofas and chairs. Lord Beresford ordered the fire brought up to life to take off the evening chill and after dinner drinks were served, while Amelia adjusted the position of the stool to her liking and familiarized herself with the piano.

Of course, they were all fundamentally the same and any amateur would say there is no difference at all, but Amelia knew every detail of her pianos and believed that each one had a unique personality. The Lady Blackburn's had a voice more like her own piano at the country house. The one she played in London, was considerably newer with a richer deeper sound. Her first chords were experimental, testing the sound to see how it differed. It was in tune, but the keys did not have the well-played feel of a frequently used piano. It had the lonely feel of an instrument that seemed to have sat for some time, untouched.

Commander Beresford was standing by the fire, leaning against the mantle just far enough from the others that he would not be expected to join in their conversation. When Amelia began to play he walked over to stand beside her, at her shoulder. Amelia, who was used to being watched so by her previous instructors, did not fumble, though she believed he had hoped to make her do so. He was close enough that she could smell the scent of his cologne.

"Do you not require sheet music?" he asked, just loud enough to be heard over her playing.

"I have many songs memorized," Amelia replied, sitting up a little straighter. She prided herself on her ability to do so. "I have been playing since I was a small child, and the music comes naturally to me. How long has it been since your mother has played?"

He thought for a moment. "I don't know. As a child, I remember her playing often, but more recently, she likes to spend her time in Bath or London. She rarely comes here. I am afraid this piano has been sorely neglected." He turned the glass in his hand and he seemed melancholy.

She wanted to raise his spirits. "Not so neglected that it is out of tune," Amelia said. "Your father must be a kind man to keep it tuned for your mother."

Amelia felt Commander Beresford stiffen beside her, the fabric of his jacket rustling.

"Oh," Commander Beresford said. "It is not for her. My father is simply a man who likes everything to be just so...in tune, I suppose. At least, neatly in its place," he finished uncertainly.

"And what about you, Commander Beresford? Do you like things to be in tune, also; in their proper place?"

"Oh, no," he said with a spark in his eye. "I am the discordant note in this house. You shall see, Lady Amelia."

He moved away from her before she could comment, but her stomach clenched with nerves.

In losing her father, she seemed to have lost some of her manners. Chastened, she focused on her playing. It was nothing more than guilt over not being a proper guest, she told herself. It did not mean anything else.

Part 3

Unlikely Engagement

11

---

*L*ady Amelia Atherton was the first to wake. The pale light of the day had just begun to creep into the room, and Amelia, always an early riser, felt anxious to begin her day. She lay in bed as long as she could, thinking about the mysterious book she had found in her father's office. The more she thought about it, the more convinced she was that her father did not just die in a carriage accident. He had been killed. How could she sleep when she had such thoughts?

She leisurely outfitted herself in a simple morning dress of black dyed muslin and a redingote with a high backed collar that opened to a vee at the front and fastened just under the bosom; to ward off the morning chill. Once dressed, she dithered with impatience. Her Aunt Ebba would sleep past noon unless something dire occurred; and if it did, she would wake so grumpily, everyone would wish she had been allowed to stay abed. Lady Patience, Amelia's friend from London, was also still abed. Her soft snores were audible through her door, so Amelia tiptoed past. She stopped at the top of the stairs, listening, but all below was silent. She felt a bit self-conscious creeping about at the early hour since she was a guest at Stanherd Residence, the Beresford's country home. Lord Percival Beresford would not mind she decided, but Commander Beresford...She thought about meeting Commander Samuel Beresford at this early hour and blushed. Still she found herself creeping down the stairs, tucking her father's book with its strange symbol beneath her arm. From a distance, the book would look like any other, she thought, and she wanted to see it in sunlight in case the brighter illumination revealed something she had missed on prior inspections by candlelight.

A few servants were awake. The fires were lit and she could hear them clanking about in the kitchen below and occasionally a burst of raised voices, but the second floor of the house was empty apart from her. She did not ring for a maid to attend her, though she was thinking fondly of tea with lots of cream, or even a warm cup of milk. It would not do for them to take special interest in her or what she was doing. The book, she knew from the secret niche, where she found it, should remain undisclosed. She went to the piano room. It seemed the abode of comfort for her, even in this unaccustomed place. Seating herself in one of the armchairs Amelia opened the book on her lap. The leather was soft from countless fingers touching it. Again, she was confronted by the sight of words, legible, normal words, but that was all they were. They were not arranged in any sentences of sense.

She tried angling it to catch the light from the window, but nothing changed on the page. It had been a farfetched hope, she knew, but this puzzle was driving her mad. None of the papers or letters in the drawer with the book had appeared to be a key to the code, but perhaps there was something she had missed. Or was she thinking far too deeply into this, and imagining a conspiracy where none existed? Could it be just a book of gibberish? Just random words in a book? No, she decided, there would be no point to that, and this book clearly took a large amount of effort to make. Someone put great care into it, and there was a reason for it. Furthermore, her father had hidden it away in a secret drawer, and that was reason enough for suspicion. Her father had never seemed a secretive man in life. Now in death, it seemed as if she may have been mistaken.

Amelia ran her fingers over the words, missing him. Oh Father, she thought. How can you be gone? How could you have left me so suddenly with no recourse? Surely you did not gamble your fortune away. There must be some logical answer, and some logical person to blame. I will find them, she promised her father's ghost. I will.

She looked at the book again. There was no texture, apart from the normal amount of indent from the printed words. She flipped to the back of the cover page; then leaned back, holding it above her head and turning the book one way, and then the other letting the early morning light shine on it. Nothing. Sighing, she lowered it again, and her heart stopped.

Commander Samuel Beresford was there, standing in

the center of the doorway with a cup of something steaming lifted halfway to his mouth. She took him in a moment. His jaw was unshaved and his hair somewhat rumpled. He was in his shirt sleeves with them rolled up past his elbows. His forearms were tanned and muscled. He wore no cravat. His Adam's apple moved as he swallowed. He seemed as surprised to see her as she was to see him.

Amelia slammed the book shut and tried to tuck it against her side, hidden from view by the side of the armchair. She shoved it into the crevice between the cushions. Belatedly, she realized how guilty a gesture that was, and quickly folded her hands in her lap. Samuel's eyes were fixed on her as he carefully sat the cup on a side table and busied himself with rolling down the sleeves of his shirt.

"Good morning, Commander Beresford. You are up early," she said, leaning against the arm of the chair in feigned nonchalance. "Is that a trait of naval life? I suppose you must get used to all sorts of odd hours, is that correct?" Her voice felt unnaturally high. Maybe he hadn't seen the book.

Samuel did not immediately respond. He picked up the cup and raised it the rest of the way to his lips and took a sip; then he took a step closer to Amelia. She found herself leaning back against the chair, pressing the book deeper down into the cushion.

"Yes," he said, simply, but he did not back up. His voice was a low rumble. "Good morning Lady Amelia. What is that book?"

Amelia had botched everything. She had wanted to

keep the book a secret in case it held some incriminating evidence against her father and then she had seemingly made the book as obvious as if it were painted a bright red. Why had she brought it out of her room? She was a fool.

"I am not sure," she answered, truthfully.

Samuel raised one dark brow. In the sunlight, she could see that his eyes, so dark she had believed them black before, were in fact a deep shade of brown, like a warm rich chocolate.

"You are reading a book you know nothing about?" he said. "Not even the title? Now that is odd." He scrutinized her over his tea cup. "Can you read? Or is that not something they teach ladies these days?"

"Of course I have been taught to read," she spat. "Do you presume the worst of everyone you meet, or is that honor solely mine?" asked Amelia, growing cross. She stood and yanked the book out of the cushion crevice, pulling the cushion with the book. It tumbled to the floor. "Oh bother," she snapped as he watched her with mild amusement as she replaced the cushion. There was no subterfuge now. She held the book out in front of her. "If you can make any sense of this, oh lauded Commander, be my guest. It is nonsense, and there is no title or author that I can discover. It is only a book of words."

"Most books are," he said dryly.

"This book is different," she said. "But I am, as you know, just a simple woman. Perhaps I am mistaken."

Samuel plucked the book from her outstretched hands with one of his, palming it easily in his long blunt fingers. He put down his cup and traced the symbol on the cover with the pad of his finger. A crease appeared between his brows.

"I know this symbol," he said, to himself.

Amelia gasped. She had not expected him to recognize it.

"You do? But how? I have never seen it anywhere else," she said, leaning toward him to see the cover again.

"I have seen this before. What are the chances of this?" He whispered, as he lifted his cup again and sipped his tea. He still had not looked at her, nor really spoken to her. She might as well not have been there at all. Amelia stifled the urge to wave her hand beneath his nose to check if she had gone invisible without noticing.

"Slim, I imagine," she said, terse. "Will you speak to me now or should I blend into the curtain and pretend I do not exist? Pray remember, that is my book, and if you are not going to tell me what it is, you can hand it back right this moment, and I will discover its meaning on my own. I was making great progress before you came along."

"I doubt that."

So he *was* listening to her, he was just choosing to ignore her. Even worse. Amelia grabbed hold of the top of the book and gave it a tug. It did not budge in Samuel's one handed grip, but he did look up at her at last. He tugged back. She took hold with both hands and wrenched, jostling the tea cup he held in his other hand, sending some of the contents spilling onto the floor.

"I am sorry about that," said Amelia, not relinquishing her hold. He was looking at her as if she had gone mad, and there was something like amusement on his face. "Let go! It is my book!" She snapped.

"Shh," he said, holding steadfast. "Or you will wake the house and everyone will know about this book, which I surmise you did not want the world to know of."

"No, I did not want you to know of it either, but here you are," said Amelia icily. She gave up on pulling the book out of his hands, they were strong and she had no chance of pulling it free from his grip. Instead she tried to stomp on his toe.

Samuel lifted his foot out of the way. Now there was no doubt about the amusement on his face, he was laughing at her! She tried again to take the book with no more luck.

"You are awful at being quiet; do you realize that?" Samuel asked. He gave the book a quick pull and yanked it free from Amelia's grasp, then lifted it over his head where she could not reach it at all, teasing her as if she were a child.

Amelia had never felt so short in her life. He was at least two heads taller than she, and with the book at the end of his long arms it might as well have been on the ceiling. She contemplated finding a new target for kicking.

"Don't," he said taking the measure of her.

She folded her arms across her chest. "It is my book," she hissed.

"So it is," he agreed without relinquishing it. "You say you know nothing at all about this book? How did you come to be in possession of it, then?"

"I found it," Amelia replied, wondering how much of

the truth to tell. She did not want to implicate her father, but if Samuel knew something she had to find out everything she could. "What do you know about it?"

"Nothing. Where did you find it?"

"In *my house*. It was hidden in one of the desks, as if whoever put it there did not want it to be found."

"You do not know whose it was? Your father's, one of the servants?" Samuel did not lower the book. Perhaps he could see her staring at it covetously.

"No, and the letter I found along with it was not written in his hand. It could be one of the servants I suppose, but they would have been quite covert to be hiding it where they did. I found it somewhat by chance," said Amelia.

"Somewhat?" he repeated.

"I was sorting my father's things," she admitted. "Where did you see the symbol prior to this? Do you have a similar book?"

"My arm is growing tired. If I lower the book down to your miniature height, will you promise not to go tearing off with it?"

"Why do you care what I do with it?" she hissed.

"I'm curious," he admitted, and continued, his voice dropping an octave. "And chasing you down would cause quite a ruckus... no matter the amusement it might bring." He lifted his shoulder in a lazy shrug but his eyes held an intensity that made her squirm. "Imagine your aunt's dismay to find me hurtling after you." He grinned at her, his face suddenly bright with mischief. "I do not think you wish to wake the entire house in such a manner. Do you?"

Amelia, feeling mulish, considered aiming a kick at his shin while he was otherwise occupied. Then, remembering she was a guest in his house and that, at one point in her life, she had been the epitome of manners. She decided against it and nodded. He came to stand beside her and brought the book down so they might both look at it. She was immediately brought up short by the heat of him as he stood close. His hands were tanned and strong as he flipped through the pages, and she couldn't take her eyes off of them. She could not help but think of the muscular arms that she had seen before he folded down his sleeves, and how easily he kept the book from her, holding her off with only one hand and little effort. She thought of that hand in hers when they had danced, before her father's death. It seemed so long ago.

"Truly, I know as much as you about this book, or rather about the symbol. I saw it once only, in my own father's study," Samuel was saying. She was brought back to the present and forced herself to concentrate. "Percival was looking at a book with the same symbol, and he was in a hurry to hide it from me when I entered," said Samuel. "It was not in as good of condition as this one though," he said. "It looked to have taken a dip in the drink," he said.

"Pardon," she said.

"It was severely water damaged," he explained. "Not so readable as this." He flipped back to the first page and Amelia watched his confusion mount as he silently read the words.

They seemed to make as little sense to him as they

had to her, for he shook his head and began the page again, and on the third time gave up, saying, "This is nonsense. Why would someone just make a list of words?"

"I have read it; the book, the papers, and none of it makes any sense. I had hoped you might have known the code for it. It must need a cypher of some sort."

Samuel flicked through the rest of the pages of the book, stopping at random to scan a section.

"There must be a purpose; I am sure of it," said Amelia.

"I agree, or no doubt, Percival would not have bothered to hide the thing. He would have said 'come have a look at this nonsense,' and we would have had a laugh."

"So you did not get a proper look? Could your brother's papers contain the cypher?" Amelia leaned closer to see the section Samuel had opened.

Her shoulder brushed against his arm and he looked down at her. She took a sharp breath, as if just realizing how close they were standing. She could smell the scent of him. She took a hasty step back, liquid heat filling her.

"No," he said, slowly, holding her gaze in a lazy way that made Amelia's cheeks flush. The man was shameless and had all the manners of a sailor. Finally he spoke, his voice low and soft. "But we could go and take a look for ourselves." His voice seemed a physical thing, drifting over her skin with a subtle promise and she shivered.

"I should...I should..." She stammered as she took yet another step back. What was she doing? She blinked at him, and then took another quick step away. The moment was broken.

"I'm sorry," she said attempting to regain her composure. "Break into Lord Blackburn's study while I am a guest in his home? Invade your brother's privacy? I should think not." Her face was aflame. "It wouldn't be proper." She finished lamely, as if any part of this situation was appropriate.

12

———

*S*amuel looked at Lady Amelia, as she stuttered, caught by his gaze. Color crept up her neck. Was she really backing out at this point? He wondered. Now, that his morning routine was already interrupted? Was she only now realizing that they were alone? She had been assaulting his senses from the moment he walked into the room. He liked to walk about the house with his tea in serene silence. She had fractured that silence and burned into the morning with the heat of a rising sun. On his ship, the *Amelia*, he had often been awake in the early hours, when only a handful of other crew had been at work, and he had grown to covet those quiet moments, watching the first rays of the sun reflect of the sea, and marveling at its beauty...at her beauty.

Samuel cleared his throat nervously. He had momentarily forgotten the papers in his father's office until he had seen the same symbol on the book in Lady Amelia's hands. Now he was reminded of the pages and his brother Percival's secretive attitude about them. He was annoyed at himself that he did not have a good answer for her. Even little details were important for a good captain to remember.

But the only details he could seem to focus on at the moment were part of Lady Amelia Atherton herself. For all her slight size, she managed to fill up the whole of his awareness. The scent of her, light and flowery lingering from the perfume she had worn to dinner the night before; her bottom lip full and pouting as she frowned at him. She was damnedly distracting. Outside of her ballroom finery, with her hair a little tousled and her dress plain, she looked ravishing. It was unfair. He had always prided himself on his self-control. He would not let a woman into his life. He had no time for one.

"I will get to the bottom of this. You should go back to sleep," Samuel said. "Don't all gentle women sleep until noon," he spat, suddenly annoyed that the course of his peaceful morning had been broken. Perhaps the Lady Amelia's very nearness was the cause of his frustration, but he chose to blame the interruption.

"I do not," she said.

Samuel did not want to argue with her; at any moment she might renew her attempts to batter his toes and shins.

"I want to know what this book is about just as much as you do, and it is mine!"

"Take it, then, I do not need it," said Samuel, tossing the book to her. She caught it narrowly, before it fell to the floor. "Go on, off to bed with you."

"I am not a child," she hissed, kicking out with her slippered foot.

This time, Samuel did not dodge her attack and she gasped in pain when her toes connected with his shin bone.

"Feel better? Now. What was that you were saying about not being a child?"

Lady Amelia's grimace was wiped from her face, replaced by a cold, hard stare that had probably knocked lesser men straight off their feet. However, Samuel had seen that sort of face on his superior officers from the age of twelve, and on his father's face since the day he was born, and it had no effect on him. Once she realized this, Lady Amelia turned on her heel and stalked away.

"Where are you going?" Samuel asked, hurrying after her.

"I am going to your father's office," said Amelia, not bothering to slow down or ask for directions. She marched down the hallway, sticking her head into all of the rooms they passed.

"You do not even know what room it is," said Samuel, incredulous. "What happened to not being a rude guest?"

"A child," she said through clenched teeth, "does not mind a little misbehaving. Ah, here we are, I think."

She pushed the door open the rest of the way and stepped into the room. Samuel followed; then shut the door behind them with a soft click. Lord Blackburn's study was untouched since Percival had last been in it, and everything was neatly put away. It was very different from Amelia's own father's study. His had a tumbled appearance though he would have known where everything was. Samuel's father's study bespoke of an utter fastidiousness. He would know if something was out of place.

"Now, where would it be?" she asked, turning toward Samuel.

If she realized that she was shut in a room alone with a strange man, it did not show on her face.

"Your guess is as good as mine, I am afraid," he said, and then paused, remembering. "A moment," he said raising a finger. "Percival was sitting at the desk with a satchel already opened when I entered." Samuel crossed the room with a purposeful stride and pulled open a desk drawer. He frowned. "I thought he tossed the whole lot into the drawer. He seems to have moved it. We shall just have to search for it," Samuel said.

Lady Amelia surveyed the room. Floor to ceiling bookshelves packed full of leather tomes similar to the one she had in her hands, and only two of them to search.

"You found the original book in a desk, so perhaps we should start there?" Samuel asked as Lady Amelia peered around at the shelves looking a little daunted before she even started. Samuel stepped closer towards her and when she looked at him again, his heart leapt into his throat. He would have taken her in his arms.

"The papers," she said, her voice sounding breathless.

He paused and decided to play the gentleman. "I will search the drawers and when I am finished with the desk, I will help you." Samuel said.

"Check for any hidden latches, that is how I found this." She replied quickly and began at the shelf to the right side of the door, working from the bottom to the top.

Samuel watched her for a moment. All of her movements were graceful, purposeful. She might have made a decent rigger, if she had been born a man. That thought drew his gaze to her curves and the slender dip of her waist, the milky white skin exposed at the nape of her neck; no, Lady Amelia Atherton was all woman. What would it feel like to touch that skin? Smooth as butter, he would bet. He should have kissed her.

"Are you going to begin looking or will you just gawk all morning?" asked Amelia, turning about with one hand on her hip quick enough to catch him staring.

Samuel tried for a charming smile, but she only scoffed and turned back to the books. A tough nut to crack, that one; not that he wanted to. No, there was nothing but trouble with women like her. He had told Percival exactly that, and yet here he was, losing his head over her.

He walked over to his father's desk. Just a few papers were stacked in a neat pile on top, Percival's work, but they were nothing more than accounts of the land. None were marked with the sigil. Then he checked all of the drawers, keeping in mind Lady Amelia's advice and searching the sides and bottoms of them for any hidden catches. Nothing. With a sigh, he sat back onto the leather chair and kicked his feet up on the desk, closing his eyes and leaning his head back thinking. Where would Percival have hidden it?

"You cannot be serious," said Amelia, her voice startling him awake. "Here you are, falling asleep, while I go over every inch of this office. Some help you are. Do you even want to find the book? Lazy man, no wonder you are not a captain!"

"I beg your pardon," said Samuel, rising from the chair. "You will take that back. I have received praise for my work ethic and ability, and everyone believes I will make captain within the year. I will not be talked down to by a woman barely old enough to be called such."

"You are all talk, *Mister* Beresford. If there is one thing I know, it is that men often are." Lady Amelia slapped her book down on the desk in front of him and went back to searching the shelves. "All talk," she spat.

He caught her arm and pulled her down on his lap. Her arms steadied herself against his shoulders, and he tasted those petulant lips with his kiss. Heat seared through him as soon as he touched her and she softened; then stiffened. He realized almost immediately this was a mistake. Her mouth was closed and chaste beneath his, and her hands were balled fists on his chest. She pulled away, and he let her. She stared at him with wide desire-filled eyes. For a moment he expected her to slap him and run from the room.

Instead she cleared her throat and said, "Are you going to help me find these papers or not, you lazy cad?"

Samuel rubbed his hand through his hair, stung.

"I have never met a lady with such a barbed tongue," he said, trying not to sound petulant.

"Have you met many ladies?" she asked.

"I am an Earl's son."

"Hmm," said Amelia, not so much as glancing at him.

"I thought you were more acquainted with a different sort of woman."

"How so?"

"Well, when you pay an incognita for her company, you pay her to say sweet things as well. Perhaps that is why none of them have told you what they truly think."

Samuel gasped. "How do you have any friends at all?" Samuel asked, shaking his head. He wished he hadn't kissed her, he told himself. His body disagreed. He dragged his fingers over the spines of the books as he read them.

Lady Amelia tensed at his remark and he could see that he had struck a nerve. He had the sudden desire to fix it, to apologize and make her smile return. He fought it down. Nothing could come of his attraction to her. She was too high born for a tumble. No for her it would be marriage...Lud! where had that thought come from?

"Where would your brother hide something he did not want you to find? Somewhere you would never look?" she asked, and her tone was pure ice, but her hands were shaking.

Samuel gave a dry laugh. "On these shelves, I assume. I rarely read, apart from the charts."

She noticed them then, a stack of scrolls, some open on the desk, all numbers and lines drawn along a map of the sea. There were virtually no words on the maps. "And how long do we have before your brother will rise for the day?" she asked.

Samuel pulled his watch from his pocket. It was an expensive gold pocket watch, although he was a second son, Amelia thought the watch was worthy of a peer and quite the gem for a sea captain, even more for a commander. "Another thirty minutes perhaps, and then he will take the time to dress properly before coming down. Breakfast is at ten, when it is just the two of us, and I expect it will be the same now."

Lady Amelia clucked her tongue and renewed her search, pulling books off the shelf, checking their covers, and then shoving them back in. "We had best hurry then. No more slacking."

"I was not slacking," Samuel protested, but he tried to match her pace. "Worse than my mother," he muttered but there was no rancor in his voice.

"I did hear that," said Amelia.

No, he thought, watching the lithe movement of the girl as she searched, she did not make him think of his mother. He turned deliberately back to his work. He wondered why he even wanted to find the papers. He had to admit to himself that although he was a little curious; the most pressing reason was simply that she wanted it.

After that, they said nothing to each other, only worked in silence side by side until the entire room had been inspected. The book was nowhere to be found, and all around them were the sounds of the house waking up. "We need to separate," Amelia said. "I cannot be found with you here."

Samuel could hear Percival's deep voice from somewhere down the hall; he seemed in conversation with a servant over the particulars of breakfast.

"Is he coming this way?" Amelia asked, anxious. She tucked her book beneath her arm and looked to Samuel for what to do. "Should we run?"

"That would look a little suspicious, I think, and you are completely incapable of subterfuge," said Samuel.

Amelia blanched. "You said Lord Beresford would not wake until near ten," she accused. "I am alone with an unwed man, and I have no chaperone. Samuel, we must think of something quickly! Oh, this would ruin me, and I would have no chance of ever marrying. I cannot recover from a mark against my name, especially without father's influence." The thought struck her with such pain she thought she would collapse. Her father's death became very real to her. Never again could she lean on her father's strong arm. "Oh, Charity would have such sport with this!" She cried dragging her thoughts from her father's death and back to her own predicament.

"Charity?" Samuel asked. "I thought your companion's name was Lady Patience."

"No, I mean yes it is. I wasn't speaking of her. Charity is... was, I suppose, a friend of mine, back in London. She was at the ball where we met, you may have seen her. Do you really not remember?"

"Oh, the ...one with..." Samuel broke off, embarrassed.

Amelia narrowed her eyes at him thinking of Charity's curvy form and her penchant for wearing dresses just a bit too low cut. "Yes, her," she snapped. "Now, focus please. What are we going to do?"

"Well, lucky for you, my brother will not believe your reputation to be besmirched in the slightest, as he knows that I will have nothing to do with any lady of quality. However, he will think it suspicious that we are in Father's office, so I suggest we walk together down the hall calmly and you allow me to do the talking if we bump into him. We are out on a tour of the house, having both risen early," Samuel said, nodding to himself.

It was a fine plan.

"I think it is best if I do not inquire as to why your brother believes that about you; I will only be offended," said Amelia, giving Samuel what he now recognized as her disgusted look. "What if he sees the book?" she hissed. "He will recognize the symbol at once. I don't have pockets and you don't have a jacket. If you were wearing a jacket like a gentleman, we could hide it under your coat."

"If you had left it in your room instead of wandering around with it, we wouldn't have to hide it." Samuel pointed out.

"I wanted to see it in the sunlight, where I thought... Oh, bother. No one knows what book it is if I hide the symbol, do they? I could say it is a book of poetry."

Samuel raised an eyebrow at her. "Very well," he said. "Come along then."

They walked sedately out into the corridor. No one was in sight. Amelia breathed a sigh of relief. "But what about finding your book, Commander Beresford?" She asked. "Where else could your brother have hidden it?"

"I haven't the faintest idea, Lady Amelia"

"He is your brother; you must know his favorite hiding spots."

"I have spent most of my life on a ship," Samuel argued. "His bedroom, maybe. Not in Father's room; Father would have none of it, and Percy knows I will never go in there."

"Then you must," said Amelia. "That is probably where it is. After all, my book was owned by my father. No doubt your father had one too. The one you saw in Lord Beresford's possession." Amelia shifted the book nervously to the other hand. "I have an idea. Patience, Aunt Ebba, and I will ask Lord Beresford for a visit to the gardens, as I have recently developed an interest in gardening. It looks to be a fine day for it. You, being a surly grump of a man, will beg off, stating that you hate flowers and all things of beauty, leaving you alone in the house to search his room and your father's room at leisure."

"I take it back," Samuel said curling his lip. "You are just fine at subterfuge."

Amelia raised her chin, all lofty proper lady once again. "Nothing I said was a lie. I do enjoy gardens and you despise anything lovely."

Oh, no, my lovely Lady Amelia, he thought. That was surely a lie.

Lady Amelia turned and walked ahead of him before he could respond, leaving him to once again chase after her. If only...but what to do with her when he caught her, he wondered.

13

Percival, as Samuel had said he would, did not so much as blink an eye when he saw Lady Amelia and Samuel together in the hallway. He was still thin from his ordeal of poisoning, but he no longer bore an air of illness about him. The faint purple shadows had disappeared from below his eyes, and he wore a welcoming smile.

His manners were impeccable, and everything that Samuel's were not. Aunt Ebba and Patience came down only a quarter hour later, and the group gathered in the dining room for breakfast.

"What is that tatty old book you are carrying about?" Aunt Ebba asked, reaching across the table to grab it from where it sat beside Amelia's plate. She had not known where else to put it, and decided that trying to hide it again would seem suspicious. She had placed it so that the symbol was facing the table.

"Just a book of poetry," said Amelia, sliding it away from Aunt Ebba's reach. "It was Father's."

"I did not know you enjoyed poetry, Amelia" said Patience. "Are you fond of poetry, Lord Beresford?"

Percival sat up in his chair. "*Speaking most plain the thoughts which do possess, her gentle sprite: peace, and meek quietness, And innocent loves, and maiden purity.*"

Patience gasped in delight. "Charles Lamb? How wonderful. Have you read his dear friend Coleridge?" she asked.

"Oh yes. Samuel Taylor," Percival clarified. "Of course, but he is so dour. My brother was named for him."

"I was not," Samuel objected.

Amelia chuckled. She could not help it, she looked across the table to Samuel and saw him with a piece of toast paused before his mouth, and the bemused expression on his face that matched her own. He caught her eyes on him and flashed a grin. Amelia shivered and slapped marmalade aggressively onto her toast.

"May we have a tour of the gardens today, Lord Beresford?" Amelia could not wait any longer, she was so anxious to solve this mystery. "It seems such a fine day for a stroll."

"It would be my pleasure. Our mother took great pride in the gardens and I believe they are some of the best in the area," said Percival.

"I must decline," said Samuel, when everyone else rose to follow Percival outside. He leaned his chair back on two legs and took a bite out of a pastry. "I will stay here and make sure none of this food goes to waste."

"Whatever will we do without you, Samuel? As I said, he cannot resist a decent meal. sailing turns men into dogs," said Percival.

Aunt Ebba, Patience, and Amelia followed Percival out of the room. Amelia turned to look over her shoulder at Samuel, aiming a meaningful look at the book she had left on the table. She hung back, letting Patience walk beside Percival.

"You have been acting strangely," said Aunt Ebba, as she came up beside Amelia. "Out with it. What is bothering you?"

Amelia, who had been thinking only of whether or not she could give Samuel enough time to find his brother's book, struggled to come up with something other than the truth. Aunt Ebba mistook her silence for sorrow. She laid her hand on Amelia's shoulder.

"Your father loved you, Amelia, and he would have wanted you to move past the grief and find happiness. With a husband," said Aunt Ebba. She always had to work an agenda. Amelia sighed.

"I know, Auntie, and I am trying," Amelia replied.

Aunt Ebba nodded toward Patience and Percival. "They are an excellent match. You would do well to find someone. See how happy Lady Patience is?"

"Patience is a simpler girl than I am, Auntie, and you know it."

"But I have seen the way you look at Samuel," said Aunt Ebba, cutting in. "He is not a proper match for you. I have seen his type before and you cannot afford a scandal."

Amelia stopped mid step, looking incredulously at Aunt Ebba. "Then your eyes are failing you. I have no interest in the man."

Aunt Ebba pursed her lips. "Say what you will, but I am not blind. I am just warning you to proceed with caution."

Amelia feigned sudden interest in a fist-sized peony. What had Aunt Ebba meant by *his type*? Although Amelia had been introduced to countless gentlemen since her debut, none of them were anything like Samuel Beresford, so she did not believe him part of a type at all. Really, it offended her that Aunt Ebba thought so little of Amelia's judgement. She may no longer be the jewel of London but that did not mean she had been brought quite that low.

Aunt Ebba had rejoined Percival and Patience in their slow promenade along the garden path. It was obvious to Amelia that, if both sets of parents were amenable to the match, the courtship between Lord Beresford and Lady Patience would be swift. The two looked at each other as if they had never before met someone so agreeable. She wished them all the best; it was a better match than she had ever dreamed of for Patience and her darling friend deserved every bit of happiness. Charity could live out her days as a spinster, for all Amelia cared. Not a single letter had she received from her so-called friend, Charity. No matter, she was better off without her. It simply stung Amelia's pride to be so forgotten.

They had nearly completed their circuit of the garden, which was small but impeccably kept, with every space filled with colorful blooms in complementary colors to the ones beside them. Despite her distracted state, Amelia had picked up a few ideas for her garden back home. Now that they had turned toward the door, however, she was entirely caught up in thoughts of the book, and whether or not she had given Samuel enough time to locate it.

SAMUEL HAD to keep reminding himself that he was being a proper younger brother now, snooping on his elder and digging through his belongings. It was something all younger brothers did, and he had missed out on his chance during his childhood days, a sentiment that only mildly assuaged the guilt Samuel felt while tossing through the bedroom. If someone had ransacked his own cabin in such a manner, he would never have forgiven them, brother or no. He could not even pretend his deception was for a worthy cause— it was nothing more than curiosity that had compelled him to uncover his brother's secrets. Percival was such an open, trusting man that seeing him trying to hide something had disturbed Samuel deeply. His interest had nothing at all to do with the fact that Lady Amelia shared the same burning desire to uncover the secret of the nonsensical book.

It was with mixed feelings, then, that his fingers closed around the worn leather cover of a satchel hidden at the bottom of Percival's closet. Something crinkled as he pulled the book out, and he scrabbled around blindly to grab the array of papers that had been dropped from and scattered beside it. Then, he heard the door open and close downstairs. Samuel climbed to his feet, checking that the room bore no obvious signs of his search. He held the satchel tightly against his chest and fled back to his own bedroom. With luck, Percival would not be looking for the papers while the three women were guests at the house, and Samuel would have plenty of time to look through the assortment and return it before Percival ever noticed it was missing.

Grateful he had always been an anti-social curmudgeon and would not attract suspicion by his absence; Samuel sequestered himself in his room and laid the damaged book and the papers out across his desk. He turned the key in the lock of the door, poured himself a brandy, and set to work. The first thing he noticed was that the books were indeed identical, inside and out, but Percy's was nigh on unreadable with water damage. The ink was smeared in many places and the pages had dried crinkled. Faint white dust on the pages told of not just water, but sea water. He brought it to his nose and sniffed. It smelled slightly musty. This book had been immersed in salt water and then inexpertly dried. It had not simply been splashed with sea water, but rather it was sitting in the water for some time, forgotten, he wondered or perhaps unable to be reached during a sea voyage?

He looked at the pages again. The loose pages from Amelia appeared to be the collection of a third book in the making. The same nonsensical words filled each page and the symbols were drawn on the same spots.

Several loose pages were poems. How did the poems and the book work together? The only thing he could see was that some of the words in the book were also rhyming words of the poems. He had never been much of a poetry sort of man, so he wasn't sure where to take this observation.

He searched for an hour, trying to make sense of the words and the letters. Samuel knew little of codes or cyphers, and his brain ached at trying to piece together a puzzle without a single idea of what the end result should look like. Was it a story? A manual? A manifest? His only breakthrough came when he was shuffling the papers back into a neat pile, and dropped one.

He took out the page and smoothed it on the desk. It was another poem, but on this one, he noticed something that was not on the others, a list of numbers at the right margin of a poem paper. It seemed to him that those numbers should mean something to him, but he couldn't think what.

But he knew the writing. It was Percy's, and he knew Percy wasn't having a secret affair. The love of his life was outside in the garden with him, but then, what was Percy doing with the cypher book? A shiver of unease went through him. What if Percival was involved in something untoward? He thought of going to their father with that news, and knew he wouldn't. He never would betray his brother. Samuel sighed. Who was he fooling? This was Percival, the prim and proper. This business had to be something else entirely. Something he wasn't seeing.

The whole thing was impossibly frustrating. Samuel had never enjoyed puzzles, he liked things clear cut and straightforward, like the sea. It was either storm or sun, and one could tell the difference readily. He thrust everything into a pile and dumped it into the drawer of his desk, not bothering to hide the papers further. If someone else stumbled upon the mess, he welcomed their attempts to solve the puzzle for him. The whole affair was giving him a headache.

As he left his room, he wondered why Percy had this book in the first place. Samuel realized he should just ask Percival. He would flat out ask him, and if Percy said it was none of his business, Samuel would insist. It occurred to him that Percival's possession of this secret may have had something to do with his poisoning. It would be just like Percy to stumble on something illegal and not even recognize the danger. He knew he could trust his brother. He just had to figure out a time to have this conversation, when Percival was feeling up to it, and the women were otherwise engaged.

SAMUEL STRAIGHTENED his cravat in the mirror and downed the last of his drink. He ran a comb through his dark hair, which had grown a bit long and a little unruly during his time ashore, and rubbed his fingers against the day's growth of hair on his chin. It was damned itchy, but he did not want the bother of sitting for a shave. It gave him a devilishly rogue look, he thought, and it would probably annoy Lady Amelia which was another plus to the shadow on his face. With a spring in his step borne of brandy and confidence, he headed downstairs to find her.

He found Percival and Lady Patience in the sitting room. Percy was reading to her, a book of poetry of course, while she embroidered something colorful. It was a disturbingly domestic scene with the two of them sitting rather close, talking in low tones. Lady Patience sat up hastily when he entered, as she nervously explained that Aunt Ebba had only gone to nap a moment ago.

Percival stood, scowling at him and laid the book of poetry aside.

"And where is Lady Amelia?" Samuel asked, amused. The girl was so fretful you would have thought he had caught them in an embrace. For the decorous pair, he may as well have, he supposed. "Did she go to lie down as well? I had something I wished to show her."

He ignored Percival's frown. His brother always assumed the worst of him.

"She went... oh, I do not know," Lady Patience stuttered, bringing her hands up to her cheeks as they heated. "Did you see, Lord Beresford?"

Percival's face was an exact replica of Patience's. Samuel did his best to stifle a laugh. "I am afraid not. I am sure Lady Amelia went up with her aunt. Yes, I believe that is what she said."

Samuel knew his brother well enough to hear the outright lie in his voice. He had been too wrapped up in Patience to pay any mind to the far lovelier Lady Amelia. Patience had a certain charm Samuel supposed, but the mouse of a girl had not half the beauty nor, half the fire of Lady Amelia. That was the trouble with love; it muddled your discernment.

"No matter. Excuse me," said Samuel, but the pair

had already forgotten him. He left the room and wandered down the hallway while Lady Patience's worries of propriety, sounded in whispers behind him.

He knew Lady Amelia would not be taking a nap. The intense woman would be waiting somewhere for him to tell her what he had found out, and would probably shake it out of him the moment she saw him. Samuel did not know why he was so looking forward to it. He trained the smile off of his face.

Lady Amelia was sitting at the piano, playing so softly it could only be heard just outside the room. Samuel stood a moment in the doorway, unnoticed, and watched her. While she played, her expression was peaceful, almost tender, and her fingers moved precisely over the keys, like a lover's hands tracing the curve of a familiar body. The song moved through him with all the imagined gentleness of the sea. There was a power beneath it that intrigued him. He did not know how long he had stood there watching her when her fingers stuttered on the keys and she turned to look at him. Her expression whipped him out of his reverie. How did she manage to turn that angelic face into one of a cross nanny?

"Are you going to come in, or just stand there in the doorway watching me?" she asked, turning back to the piano. She started playing again, but it was a different song than the song of longing she had been playing before he entered.

"What was the song you were playing?" He stepped into the room and shut the door behind him, leaning back against the wood, arms crossed over his chest. "I have never heard it before."

"You would not have. I wrote it myself, but it is a work in progress, and not yet ready for an audience," she said, with a slight shake of her head. Her dark curls fell forward, obscuring her face, but he had seen a shadow creep over her expression.

"It sounded ready," Samuel argued. "It is quite beautiful."

Amelia stopped playing and shut the lid of the piano with a snap. She swiveled on the bench to face him, crossing one leg elegantly over the other, a motion that revealed a flash of black stocking. Samuel cleared his throat.

"Do they educate sailors in music theory, now? That must be a new addition to the curriculum," she said, with that arrogant tilt to her chin that had so amused him on first meeting.

"I am still the son of an Earl," Samuel said, pushing away from the door and standing to his full height. "Even if I am the second son."

"And that drives you mad, does it not? That you are the second son?"

"Whatever do you mean?"

"You think you hide your jealousy so well, playing it off with that devil may care attitude and nonchalance, but I can see right through you, Commander Beresford." Amelia put her elbow on the piano, leaning against it so her hip cocked out to one side. He teetered a moment between anger and desire, and then, Samuel stalked toward her, looming over her, but she did not recoil nor so much as bat an eye.

"I would never wish for my brother's life," said

Samuel. "It is nothing but boredom and duty and manners. No adventure, no thrill. Percival is the one suited to it."

"So you say," said Amelia, tone and expression bored as she pursed her lips, and then wet them. "But you wish you had at least had the option, do you not?"

Samuel did not know what to say; it was too near the truth. It wasn't that he wanted his brother's life though. He didn't. He was entirely unsuited to it. He supposed at one time he wanted his father's approval though. He had never thought himself transparent before, but this girl had seen right through him. Unnerving. It was no longer important. He was his own man. He fumbled for a way to recover himself.

"You are nothing but a spoiled Duke's daughter. Once your life of shopping and parties was thrown off course, you realized there was nothing of substance to hold on to. So you decided to throw yourself into investigating a mystery, just to give your bored little mind something to do," said Samuel.

Lady Amelia got to her feet in a swish of silk. The gesture, which she seemed to have meant as intimidating, was rather endearing as the top of her head came only to his chest and she had to crane her head back to glare at him. Looking down at her, curls askew, eyes shining with emotion, he had the sudden desire to kiss her again. So he did.

Samuel caught her by the waist and pulled her against him, bending to once again capture her lips with his own. They were parted with her gasp of surprise. She did not slap him or pull away, but melted into him, yielding and pliant, her hands up between them, on his chest. His sudden fire mellowed to gentleness. For all her bravado, she was small and soft and he had an intense desire to protect her. Instead he kissed her with all the tenderness he had in him.

14

*A*melia had clearly lost her mind. She could not in this precarious stage of her life, lose her wits over a man she hardly knew, and who was certainly no good for her. Her feelings were easy enough to stamp down when he was not there, huge and solid and warm and kissing her so, so thoroughly that fire was exploding in her and her knees were wobbling. He held her so confidently; he surely kept her from falling. It was only when he pulled back and his arm dipped down from her waist that her mind finally decided it could function again. She took a deep cleansing breath.

"Now, enough of that." she said, shaking her curls back out of her face and stepping out of his reach. His arm slid reluctantly off of her. She willed herself to composure. "Did you find the book?" She asked.

Samuel's tender expression, something she had not seen before, snapped off his face and turned into a scowl. She was positively infuriating. How could the woman respond to him one minute and be completely unmoved the next? If it were not for the pink shade of her lip he would have believed he had imagined the entire kiss. She pressed her hands together, trying to still their shaking, hoping he didn't notice how he unnerved her.

"I did," he said, voice hoarse. He cleared his throat and tried again. "They are identical except that Percival's copy is in much worse shape than yours. The papers I found with the book were written in the same manner, more nonsense, and poetry"

Amelia's face fell. She had truly believed finding another book would somehow unlock the secret of her own.

"And there was no cypher? Nothing to help you decode the words?" she asked, already knowing the answer. He would have told her straight away. Still, he could have missed something. She wanted to look herself.

Samuel shook his head. "But there was something. I do not know if it means anything."

"What was it?" said Amelia, unable to keep the excitement from her voice.

"I'm thinking the book is the cypher," he said.

She frowned. "So you did find something?"

"Numbers. Only numbers. Written across the right margin of one of the papers," Samuel said, scratching the unseemly stubble on his face.

"Whatever could that be? It must mean something." Amelia sat at the piano tapping her foot and thinking. "We must figure this out. No doubt this is the key to the whole mystery." She just knew it was so.

"It is probably nothing more than a lovers' meeting spot, you realize," he said. "Some hidden affair. A spot at some ball..."

"You do not believe that," Amelia argued. "An affair does not require books of coded language-- Especially not multiple copies!" Amelia frowned at the look on his face.

"You've thought of something," she said.

He didn't answer.

"This is *my* mystery," she argued. "Tell me."

He still said nothing, but she was quite sure he had deduced some part of the riddle but he was not divulging it. She pursed her lips wondering if she could trust him and finally decided she had no choice.

"There is talk in London," she said. "Some say my father was involved in something untoward." She shook her head. "My father would never do something like that. He was somehow taken advantage of. Before he died," she confided, "He was worried about something one day, and then next day, he was ...he was gone. I think..." she hesitated saying the actual words. Her voice dropped to a whisper. "I think his death was no accident. I have to follow this to the end. Surely you see that. If this can clear my father's name...find the truth," she said. "Or find his murderer."

"All the more reason for you to stay out of this," he snapped.

She gaped at him. He believed her. He did not say she was irrational or call her a hysterical woman and try to placate her. No. He said to stay out of this; whatever this was. What had he found out?

"It is too dangerous," he continued pacing away from her.

"I care not a fig," she said airily. "If you are frightened, just give me the information you have deduced. I will ferret out the rest of the puzzle."

"I am not frightened," Samuel said, with a snort. "And you will not go alone. I forbid it."

"You forbid it! Are you my protector now?" Amelia's voice had an edge to it, and she stood to face him, but Samuel grinned at her, his mood changing in a moment.

"You could not pay me to take that job," He teased, his voice was suddenly jovial again, the scowl of earlier, completely wiped from his face as if it had never been.

Amelia was not fooled. She looked at him and a shiver ran down her spine, but she persevered. She clicked her tongue in annoyance. "What is it?" she asked. "I deserve at least that much. You cannot keep it from me."

"I just realized what the numbers were, and why they seemed familiar. It is latitude, and I recognized it because it is in London," said Samuel. "Or at least could be."

"Where in London? What do you suppose it is?"

"I'm not sure," Samuel said. "I suppose I can go to London to investigate, although I do not see what good it will do."

"*We* can go to London," she said.

"You are not going," he said.

"I most certainly am," she argued. "And immediately. I need to know the truth."

"You have no idea if these books will help. They may mire your father's name even further."

"How dare you say that!" she fumed. "My father was a good man."

"Even good men make a mull of it from time to time."

"You should know," she snapped.

"You don't know what this is about," he argued ignoring her jibe. "Until we know more, I cannot involve a lady."

"That is exactly why I must go!" She realized her voice was raised, and if the family came back, they would be caught. "I must go," she said again in a furious whisper. "I want to go!"

"I don't give a tinker's damn what you want," he said in the same low whisper.

She stared at him for along moment and then said with ice cordiality, "My aunt and Patience and I have imposed on your hospitality too long. We will be leaving for home in the morning."

"You are going to do harm to the happiness of your friend and my brother, just to satisfy your pride," he snapped. "You are a cruel woman."

"Good day, Commander Beresford" she said. She had to find some way to go to London and figure this out on her own. Without his book and without his help, it was going to be doubly difficult, but she would do it. She raised her chin a little. "I will do this myself if I must."

"Really?" he said smugly. "I'm sure you can discover the location with only the latitude."

"I can," she said.

He laughed at her. "No you can't."

"I can search just as well as any man," she said hotly.

"I have no doubt you can, but man or woman, latitude is only half of the equation, not the whole location."

"Oh," she said deflated.

"In any case, this has become far too dangerous, Lady Amelia."

"You don't know that," she reasoned.

And he didn't, but he surely had his suspicions, especially considering that the writing on the letter looked like Percy's shaky after illness scrawl.

Truly, Percival's poisoning was just one more reason why he wanted to steer Amelia clear of this whole mess, if she was right about her father's death then someone had murdered the Duke of Ely just on the heels of the ball where Percy was poisoned...He decided he would have to chectk the poem again.

"I'll speak to Percival," he began.

"No!" she cried. "I don't want anyone else involved."

"He is already involved," Samuel said.

"You had no right." She was fuming. She advanced on him, stomping her foot in anger.

"I had every right," he said. "These are *Percy's* papers we have been rooting through. And I now believe they are the reason why someone attempted to poison him."

"What?" She sank down in the nearest chair, white as ice. She did not swoon, but this was as close as Samuel had ever seen her to it. He didn't know if he should have told her, about Percy's near death from poisoning, and surely he could have been more tactful, but at least he had exonerated himself from her wrath.

She understood now why he needed to tell Percy what they had found, and perhaps she would not be so set on putting herself in danger, once she knew that the danger was not just supposed but a certainty.

"He was to speak with your father on the night of the ball," Samuel said. "They spoke briefly and agreed to meet on some matter of finance. Then Percy began feeling ill and we went home. We had thought it was a bad lamprey at the time, but the doctor agrees now, that it likely was a purposeful poisoning."

Amelia said nothing. She sat for a moment as if in shock and then got up and sat at the piano. After a few minutes she laid her hands on the keys and began to plunk out a slow dirge. Samuel sat with her for a while, and when he began to think she would rather be alone, he quietly left the room, and allowed her to bury herself in the music.

THE NEXT MORNING dawned with a torrential downpour, and even if Amelia had still wanted to leave, she knew Aunt Ebba was not going to travel on such a miserable day. Amelia spoke in clipped tones at breakfast, and let Aunt Ebba and Patience carry the conversation. Soon after, Aunt Ebba and Patience settled with their needlepoint in the parlor while Percival read to them. Amelia was much too nervous to sew. She would probably stick herself with the needle, and bleed on the fine silk thread. She didn't find sewing a bit relaxing at the best of times, now with her nerves on edge, her needlepoint would be a ghastly mess. Her hands were not steady enough to darn a sock.

She had barely slept thinking of what Samuel had told her. She had thought that there was foul play, with her father's death, but to have that reality confirmed shook her. To think that Lord Beresford, the man Patience so obviously loved, could have been poisoned; it was a shock. She sat looking out at the rain, thinking of all that had happened since her father's death.

"You are not playing," Samuel said as he stood at the doorway. He gestured at the piano.

"No," she answered. "I was thinking of all you told me yesterday. This is all the more reason why we must go to London."

Samuel walked into the room with a purpose. "You are a woman, a lady besides" he said. "You cannot be involved in such dangerous activities."

"I must," she said. "We cannot leave the blackguard loose to prey on some other poor unsuspecting victim."

"Leave this to me. I will get to the bottom of it," Samuel suggested gently.

"Alone?"

"Yes."

Amelia glowered at him. Samuel tried to reason with her, but Amelia was stubbornly insistent that she could do whatever a man could do and if she had to she would get to the truth herself without him. He was quite sure the woman was stubborn enough to try. The heat of their arguing brought the heat of their attraction to mind, but both of them studiously avoided the subject and Amelia returned to the matter at hand.

"Why were they targeted?" She asked, hands on her hips as if she could not see why he did not have a ready answer. She fired another question and another. "Do you have any idea? What did the villains want? Did they get it?"

"I don't know," Samuel said.

"I thought you were investigating."

"Very well," he had said dumping the entire contents together on the side table. "I'm quite sure Percival is too taken with Lady Patience to notice the books absence. See what sense you can make of it, then."

"I will," she said, raising her chin a little. Her hazel eyes flashed fire and Samuel thought she looked remarkably beautiful. He would have attempted to kiss her again but in her present mood, with her hands clenched in fists at her side, he was certain that kissing her would involve risk to his face, so he simply stalked unsatisfied from the music room.

She gathered up the satchel and papers and went to her own room. Samuel thought the rainy day felt especially silent without her piano music drifting through the hall.

IT HAD BEEN two days now since Samuel had kissed Amelia. He'd kissed her twice and now it was as if it had never happened. But it did happen. Yes, that first kiss they could both deny. It was a mistake. A woman was allowed one mistake was she not? She had not taken him to task for his impertinence because she was so startled. It was a single moment of passion, not to be acknowledged or repeated... only it was repeated, and again she had not protested. If she was honest with herself, she still could not protest. Like some low hoyden, she'd wanted it repeated.

She could not keep from thinking about his kisses and, even dreaming of them at night, but Samuel treated her no differently than he had before. He had proclaimed no words of love and devotion. He had not asked for her hand in marriage, not that she would marry him had he asked. He was only a commander, but he had said nothing...nothing at all. Was he truly unmoved? Amelia retired early and sat beside her bed looking at the book and the papers and trying to put Samuel out of her mind. She had a good portion of candle, so she thought she could stay up for an hour or two reading and trying to decipher the code. She would put herself to the task at hand. She wasn't going to sleep anyway but she had trouble keeping her mind on the book.

Her hand went to her lips as she thought of Samuel. How could he kiss her like that ...did it mean nothing? What had she been expecting, for him to follow her around like a lovesick puppy? No, but she had hoped he would... Did she? She did not know. She'd once had all manner of puppy dog men, flattering popinjays the lot, and she had rejected all of them. Now she had less choice, and ...oh what did she want? Perhaps her heart was just wishing he would kiss her like that again. Her mind however, was crafting a way she could convince him to take her to London to solve the mystery her father's death and its connection to the book with the strange symbol. Surely they could find some answers in London. She felt so useless here in the country.

She ran her finger over the symbol and studied the numbers which Samuel had given her. Somehow, those numbers were the key to figuring out what the rest of the message might be. The book was still just a book of words, not sentences. Upon closer inspection she noticed that a great number of the words rhymed with each other, and the papers, had poems...She felt a sudden wave of excitement. What if the poems were not the key; what if the book was actually the cypher as Samuel thought? On a whim, she looked back at the poem. Samuel had said the numbers were written down the right side of the paper, and the last words on the right of the paper were the rhyming words of the poem. It was nearly impossible with Percy's smeared and unreadable book, but with her own, the cypher suddenly made sense. The numbers were the pages and lines where the words were in the book.

She wanted to jump and run to Samuel to show him what she discovered, but he was probably in bed by now. The thought sent a shiver through her as she thought of him. She forced her mind back to her work.

She was not an adept with such things, but Samuel seemed to understand it. He seemed to read the numbers like an address. If they had an address she could go to London and confront whoever was at that location. She would find out what they knew about her father's death. She would not rest until justice was done.

She could barely contain her excitement. She just knew this mystery had something to do with her father's death. She just knew it! Her father had found the book and unlike her, he knew what it was. He threatened to take the culprit to the authorities and was killed for it. She knew her father was a man of honor, but proving it would have to wait until morning. She blew out the candle and forced herself to lay still in the dark. If she lay still, she would fall asleep, she told her racing mind, but once again her thoughts went to Samuel and sleep would not come.

They would need to go to London. Aunt Ebba would help; Amelia was sure of it. It would be difficult to go to London now, with her current financial problems and her uncle dogging her every farthing, but she would persevere. Her uncle would not allow it, especially if she was a woman alone, and she could not take Patience into danger...but... A plan began to take form in her mind. Her uncle need not be the man responsible for her in London, if Samuel would agree.

15

*A*melia slept fitfully and awoke early. Thankfully, Aunt Ebba was still asleep. She had dodged all of Aunt Ebba's attempts to pin her down about the time she was spending with Commander Beresford. She could not miss the knowing looks Aunt Ebba threw her way whenever Amelia was speaking to him. Her aunt was reading far too much into the situation, but perhaps that too would be useful. Samuel was but a means to ferret out the mystery surrounding her father's debts and death. He was not a suitor. He was nothing more than a lighthearted distraction, something Amelia had been desperate for since her father had passed away: a distraction and now, a way to find answers. A niggling voice in the back of her mind reminded her of those stolen kisses, but Samuel had been unaffected by them, she would do no less. She would concentrate on her father.

She went to the music room, but Samuel was

nowhere in sight. She had begun to enjoy their early morning conversations, and felt disappointed that he was not there going over his maps. She wanted to share her theory with him.

She consoled herself with music. She concentrated on the piano, on the music. Music was solid. Music settled both her mind and her heart. She played one of father's favorite concertos by rote, letting her mind wander; remembering when she had thought her father was invincible.

She stopped playing when she finished the piece. She had yet to break her fast, and she heard voices in the morning room: Her aunt, and Patience. She heard a male voice as well, but it was Lord Beresford, not Samuel. Amelia went to join them.

The morning dragged on, and Amelia was still uncertain what to do. She wanted to talk to Samuel and endeavor to convince him to take her to London or at least share with him her work on solving the cypher, but Commander Beresford had not appeared at breakfast. She expected that she could find him, but not with Aunt Ebba and Patience at her side. Finally, Aunt Ebba, Patience, and Lord Beresford had gone out to visit the stable; Amelia begged off.

"You know how horses and hay make me sneeze," she said. "I will stay in and practice my piano."

"Amelia," her aunt began, but Patience laid a hand on her aunt's shoulder. "We will speak later," Aunt Ebba said giving Amelia a solid stare.

Amelia immediately planned to use the opportunity of privacy to ferret out Samuel's hiding place and ambush him. She found him, strangely enough, in the music room. She gave him the numbers she had worked out the night before and although he said little, she thought he recognized these numbers as well as the others.

"It is a longitude, is it not?" she asked. "With both latitude and longitude we can go to London and find the culprits that killed my father."

"You are jumping to conclusions," Samuel protested.

"You cannot think my father was involved in these machinations by choice!" she said incredulously.

"Keep your voice down," he warned. "Your aunt will hear you, and wonder what mischief I have done."

"She is at the stables chaperoning Lord Beresford and Patience."

He looked at her for a long moment. "Her chaperoning skills may be misplaced," he said.

She blushed prettily and sat at the piano. She ran her fingers lightly over the keys. "I'm sure you will be the perfect gentleman," she said.

"Whatever have I done to give you that impression," he asked.

She faltered and hit an off note. Amelia played the piano as she talked, hoping it would muffle the sound of their voices so the servants who may be nearby could not be privy to their conversation. "You know what we must do in order to make this work, I hope?"

Samuel ignored her question. Actually, he enjoyed her playing. In some way the music reminded him of the sea, rising and falling with soothing waves. He was listening. He had his elbows on the desk, head bent, studying a chart.

"Is that the map?" she asked, moving to look annoyingly over his shoulder. "Will it tell us how to find the villains involved?"

"No," he said dryly. "It is just some promising bit of sea." He pointed to a spot on the map. "The ships that pass through here are loaded down with valuables, silks and spices and gold."

"Pirate!" she said and he grinned. She was close enough to kiss. Dare he steal another?

He tapped his fingers on a point on the map, holding his place, and looked up. "Shall we dress all in black then?"

"You mock me, sir," she said petulantly.

"Never! We should only disguise our faces?" he teased. "Be incognito," he said, his voice a low purr.

The double meaning of incognito, meaning disguised, and incognita, a lady of loose virtue, made her blush. "You presume too much, sir," she said haughtily, but she could feel the flame of her face, and looked away. "You are no gentleman," she said as she went back to the safety of her piano.

He followed her. "Perhaps you guessed my true identity the first time," he said.

"I do not understand."

"Perhaps I am a pirate," he whispered, "seeking to steal this treasure." He tilted her head back to kiss her. Her hands froze on the keyboard, and she could think of nothing but the kiss, the gentle warmth of him and the movement of his lips on hers. I am captured, she thought.

He released her lips and she could not pick up the threads of their previous conversation. Her fingers automatically moved on the keyboard, picking up the melody of the song she had been composing for the sea... the song for him. In a few moments she could breathe normally again.

At last she remembered what she wanted to say to him. "About the numbers," she began. "Is it in London?"

"I believe so."

"In order for us to go to London together...we must be...be..." She struggled to say the words. She had this all planned out last night. It seemed like such a good idea. Why could she not say the words?

"Be circumspect?" Samuel asked.

Amelia shook her head. "Don't be ridiculous." She could not believe she was the only one to have thought of it, nor that she had to say it aloud. She was a woman. She could not travel to London alone with a man not her relative or her betrothed. He knew that. At least she did not have to look at him as she said it. She looked at the keyboard. Although she rarely had to glance at the keys when she played, she concentrated mightily now.

"We must pretend to be betrothed," Amelia said, swallowing down the lump in her throat. Her face flamed red again. The heat of it felt like a winter hearth against her cheeks. She took a breath and peered at him.

Samuel's face had gone sheet white, so obvious she could see it from the corner of her eye. She focused even more forcefully down at her fingers, moving over the keys, though she had not the need to look as she played for over ten years now she watched the ivory as if she were a novice.

"Why in heaven's name should we do such a thing?"

He stood and paced away from her. He was incredulous, a note of strain in his voice she had never heard before, as if the idea were beyond his wildest dreams. Or, more likely in his case, nightmares. "Absolutely not. I will not."

Amelia sighed and paused in her playing. She turned earnestly to him. It was no different than being with Charity and Patience and having to explain every detail of her plans in order for them to make sense to their lesser intellects, only with the girls, she felt much more in control. Now, she felt as if she were walking along one of his ships in a storm. She took the sail in hand and plunged forward.

"I cannot be seen cavorting about London with a bachelor. I have a reputation to maintain, Commander Beresford, and with the recent... drama surrounding me, people will only be ever more interested in my behavior. We must be betrothed, and perhaps on the pretense of looking for a townhouse in London," said Amelia, the plan coming together in her mind. "You will propose to me and I will accept, and then we will put out an announcement. Shortly after that, no one will bat an eye when we arrive in London, except to gossip that I have settled sorely below my station."

Samuel's mouth was opening and closing, but no words were coming out. If it had not been the idea of marrying her that had struck him dumb, Amelia would have found it amusing. As it was, she was growing offended. Really, all the other men in the world would be jumping for joy at the news and here he was, a mere naval commander, acting as if she had requested he cut off a limb. She went back to playing, her fingers rather aggressively attacking the keys.

"It will be a charade, of course," said Amelia, practicing playing fortissimo. Her fingers pounded the keys now, taking some of her anger with the sound. "The moment we have our answers, I will call off the engagement."

"A moment then," said Samuel, finding his tongue again. He laid his hand on hers. A jolt passed through her. "Why should you be the one to call it off?"

"It would be far more believable if I were to do it. No one will ever believe you, a commander and a second son, would really back out of a marriage to a duke's daughter," said Amelia, hardly believing she had to explain this to him.

"Do not pretend your status has not diminished of late," said Samuel, crossing his arms over chest. "It makes more sense if I back out because you are too difficult or demanding or full of yourself. Anyone who has ever met you will believe that."

"Do you say hurtful things without realizing it, or do you do so intentionally?" Amelia asked, stung. She was none of those things. Maybe a little demanding, but she knew that it was the only way to go through life. Being soft gained little. One could see that by looking at Patience...at least that is what she had always told herself.

"I could ask you the same question, but I expect your answer is the same as mine; a little of both," said Samuel.

Amelia was doubly offended, because it was true, and because he had said so to her face. She lifted her chin.

"It does not matter which one of us breaks it off," said

Amelia, though it was the furthest thing from the truth. "We can work out the details later. I cannot be married while mourning my father in any case. So we need not be rushed, but there is so much to do between that time and now if we would find my father's killer."

"You truly think he was killed?"

"I do," she said. "When should we leave for London?

"Now you are just assuming I will go along with this plan and propose," said Samuel.

"Is there any other way to do what we need to do? Please, tell me if you know of one, as the last thing I would ever wish for is to be betrothed to you," said Amelia. "But if there is something in the books which can resolve this mystery and absolve father, I must find it. Surely you see that."

Samuel looked at her for a moment. He could think of one simple way to solve this problem. He could go to London alone, find out what this business was, and then tell her or not as it suited him, but the pink flush still visible on her face intrigued him. How far was she willing to take this charade? The thought amused him.

Samuel sighed, feigning compliance. "Very well. Should I do it while your aunt is here? And what of your uncle?"

"My uncle?" Amelia said.

"The *current* Duke of Ely?" he reminded her.

Addressing him so brought a lump to her throat, but she had thought of him, reluctantly, but she had thought of him. "We will have to speak to him while we are in London. I am sure he will have no objections as marrying me off means he has one less issue to deal with. He said as much. As for Aunt Ebba..." Amelia bit her lip. There was no way around it; Aunt Ebba had to be deceived just like everyone else. "We should do it before I return home. Then, we will make the journey to London together."

Samuel's impish grin gave tell to the sort of hellion he must have been as a child. "Now that I have warmed to the idea, I think this will be a fine bit of fun before I return to life at sea. Dupe all of London and stir up a scandal? Percival will never forgive me," he said, with glee.

His wholehearted acceptance of the plan filled Amelia with new doubts. "Please remember the purpose of this charade," she said. "Do not get carried away."

Samuel grinned. Oh he had every intention of being carried away, he thought. He crossed the room with his long stride and knelt suddenly by her side. He grabbed her hand and pulled it to his mouth, kissing it softly. "My heart, my love, it is too late for caution. Your beauty is like an ocean, and I have fallen, surely to drown," said Samuel, his lips quirked, but somehow he managed to keep a straight face.

Amelia pulled her hand free, her pulse jumping in her throat. The warmth of his lips lingered on her ungloved skin. She could feel the roughened skin of his hand under hers and the touch of his hand was somehow even more sensual than the kiss on her lips.

"It must be believable," Amelia said, pulling her hand out of his and folding her hands in her lap. "No one would believe that sort of behavior from you."

Samuel put one hand on the bench Amelia was sitting on and leaned toward her until his mouth was beside her ear. The tickle of his breath made her shiver. "Is this not believable, Amelia? Are you not wooed?"

Amelia's body was melting toward him, even as her mind attempted to snap her back to her senses. She bolted upright, upsetting the bench with a clatter. Samuel rose smoothly to his feet, his impish grin gone straight to devilish, but she was gratified to see, from the rise and fall of his chest, that he was not entirely immune to his own tricks.

"Announce it tonight," Amelia said, backing away an extra step, putting a little more space between them so she was not tempted to strike him... Or throw herself into his arms again. "At dinner," she said again, an edge of steel coming into her voice.

Samuel bowed at the waist. It was a perfect imitation of a polite bow, but filled with mockery, and his eyes never left Amelia's face. "As you wish, my dear *Amelia*," said Samuel purposely dropping her title.

Amelia shook her head at him. "I have not given you leave to use my given name," she said primly.

"If we are engaged, I think we should be on a first name basis, Melly my dear," he argued.

No one had called her Melly since she was a child, but scolding him would only let him know that he had gotten to her. "Very well," she said. "You may call me *Amelia* when you propose. And comb your hair before you do so, or no one will believe me when I accept."

She forced herself to walk calmly from the room, but the heat of his gaze on her back made her want to run. Her stomach was filled with fluttering butterflies and she could not stop trembling. What had she done?

The Duke's Daughter

Part 4

London Reprise

16

---

*L*ady Amelia Atherton outfitted herself in the finest dress she had brought to the Beresford country estate, and wished it was something a little more grand. She had not been expecting an occasion like this, a proposal. Even though she knew it was false, her nerves jittered and her heart raced. The dress was worn over a sarnet slip still black but, gauzy and sheer, and embroidered with black on black flowers at the hem. Puffed sleeves left her arms bare until her gloves began at the elbow. A maid fixed her tortoiseshell comb atop her head, before the mass of curls, and clasped a simple pendant of jet around her neck. There. It was the best Amelia could do as she was still in mourning after the death of her father.

"You look marvelous Amelia," said Lady Patience, her closest friend, who was also dressed for dinner with the Beresford brothers.

"Thank you, Patience," said Amelia, turning away from the mirror and taking a deep breath. "As do you. Lord Beresford will be besotted, if he is not already so. How goes your flirtation with him? You two have seemed quite taken with each other."

Patience tugged at her glove and then worried over her hair, which was a bright red with riotous curls. "I do not wish to get my hopes up. He is the son of an Earl. It still seems so... wondrous, that a man like him would ever desire me."

Amelia patted Patience's shoulder. "Only because you do not see yourself properly. You are kind and well-bred. Any man would be happy to have you. Come along now, or we will be late to dinner."

Amelia knew if she did not go down those stairs right that minute she was going to lose her nerve, throw herself down on her bed, and refuse to move. Lord Percival Beresford, eldest son of the Earl of Blackburn and his brother Commander Samuel Beresford were already downstairs in the parlor. Her Aunt Ebba was with them, laughing over something one of them had said. All eyes turned toward Patience and Amelia when they entered the room. If Amelia had not been watching Samuel so carefully, she might have missed the way his eyes widened when he saw her, and the way he had to swallow before he spoke his greeting. He held out his arm to escort her to supper. Patience sat beside her next to Lord Beresford, who had the head of the table. Amelia sat across from Commander Beresford and Patience almost immediately engaged Aunt Ebba in conversation. They had apparently brought in some rose cuttings and were admiring one another's arrangement of the flowers. The table was indeed impressive with a fine array of dishes.

"The flowers are quite lovely," Amelia demurred. "I shan't have the patience to grow such beautiful blooms I am sure," she said as the footman ladled the artichoke soup.

Patience entreated her to come to her home and practice so that she might cultivate a fine garden.

Amelia was noncommittal. She felt nothing but nerves and exchanged a glance with Commander Beresford who had the temerity to grin at her across the table. She applied herself to cutting her venison into tiny bites, which she pushed around her plate.

Time seemed to pass in a blur. Dinner tasted like ashes in Amelia's mouth. She ate enough to be polite from each course, and drank far more wine than she would normally indulge in, and wished the spinning sensation in her mind was due to the wine rather than the thought of what Samuel was about to do. No, what they were about to do.

When the meal was cleared away and dessert, a towering pyramid of fruit and marzipan had been picked over, Samuel rose from his chair. Percival followed, assuming it was time for the after dinner drinks. Amelia also stood. Legs wobbling, she pushed back her chair and rose to her feet, taking small, careful steps towards Samuel. How could the distance between chairs feel like miles? He took the distance in two long steps, and when she was at last beside him, he found her hand and took it between both of his. She knew she was squeezing too hard, grasping at him to keep her standing, but he did not pull away. Instead, he seemed to lend her some of his strength.

"Samuel," Percival began, looking from Amelia to his brother and back again. "What is all this then?"

Patience had her hand up in front of her mouth and Aunt Ebba's pursed lips said more than words ever could.

Amelia suddenly wanted to put a stop to the whole charade. This was not the way a proposal of marriage was supposed to be enacted. She wanted a genuine proposal; not from the brash Samuel Beresford, but from someone gentile, and kind and heroic: from someone who loved her. Samuel would make a muck of it, but there was no stopping it now.

"This will come as a surprise to all of you, much as my feelings for Amelia came as a surprise to me," Samuel said. "Our few days together have been all I need to realize she is the woman I wish to spend my life with, and we wish for your blessing upon our marriage," said Samuel, and he sounded so earnest that even Amelia, knowing the lie, could not find it in his words. "But we will carry through with it regardless, sailing to Greta Green if you do not approve, so really, it is pointless to argue."

Amelia grimaced. Is that what he considered adding his own personal touch? Lud, could he truly be so uncouth?

Patience had now raised both hands to her mouth and tears were falling freely over her cheeks. Aunt Ebba's lips were nothing more than a thin pink line. Percival's mouth had fallen open in shock. The room seemed to be lacking air. Then Percival stood and seized his brother into a hug, wrapping Amelia in beside him a moment later. It was done, she thought. Well, it was only temporary. She could manage for a few months. She had plenty of time to call the thing off, considering she would be wearing black for at least another five months.

"I am so happy for you both," said Percival. "Surprised is putting it mildly, but do not mistake my shock for disapproval. I support this wholeheartedly and will do everything in my power to persuade Father to do the same. Oh Samuel, how could you have kept something like this from me? Never mind, it does not matter now. I am happy for you."

Suddenly Patience was there, throwing herself around Amelia in a violent hug and sobbing against the sleeve of her dress. "You are in love! Oh, I knew it would happen and now it has! You will be the most stunning bride the world has ever seen, Amelia."

"Thank you, Patience, and you, Lord Beresford," said Amelia, patting Patience on the back until the girl released her. Tears must be contagious because Amelia was beginning to feel their threatening presence behind her eyes. I could not be moved by emotion, she told herself. No. It was only frustration that she could not simply enact the trip to London alone: frustration that she needed to involve Samuel Beresford at all.

Aunt Ebba, the last barrier, got to her feet. She did not hurry over, or pull Amelia into a hug, or begin crying. Instead, she fixed Samuel to the spot with a stare.

"Commander Beresford, you have done what no

other man has ever managed to do. You have won the heart of Lady Amelia Atherton," she said, voice cool. "Do not go breaking it."

Samuel nodded solemnly. "I would not dare, Madam" He caught Amelia's eye and sent her a singularly charming smile, as if they were truly in love. Amelia studied the tablecloth. How had this endeavor gotten out of her control?

Aunt Ebba went back to her seat and waved a footman over to pour her more wine.

"No, no more of that, there should be champagne! Bring up the finest bottle we have," said Percival, to the servants. He was nearly tearful himself. "My brother, my little brother, has found love."

Samuel, who still had hold of Amelia's hand, gave it a gentle squeeze, and Amelia found she could breathe again. "Thank you all for your support, it means so much to both of us." She said softly.

She glanced around at the faces of her friends, so open and happy for her, and then at Samuel whose eyes were twinkling as if he were enjoying a grand joke. She felt a queer unsteadiness, as if the world had just tilted. She was suddenly not so sure that this ruse was the best path.

PERCIVAL CORNERED Samuel the moment the three women had gone to bed. Percy had partaken in more than his usual amount of alcohol with his celebratory glasses of champagne, and the effect was to make him even more emotional than normal. Samuel, still sober, found it amusing. He was also glad that at last Percy seemed to have regained his appetite, both for food and wine.

"How could I not have seen the signs?" Percival asked, making his way over into a chair and collapsing bonelessly on top of it.

"Now that you have revealed your affections, it is obvious how much love there is between the two of you, the way you look at each other and smile. The way you both kept slipping away. Oh, it is so romantic; I am overjoyed for you. Have you told father?"

"Not yet," said Samuel. "I was hoping to wait a little. Lady Amelia is not quite ready to meet him. He can be intimidating, you know."

In truth, Samuel was hoping to put off telling his father long enough that he would never need know. The Earl of Blackburn was not one to read the society section of the newspaper and the whole affair could be over and done with without his father the wiser. In the end it would save Samuel the embarrassment of telling father why she ended the engagement.

Percival frowned. "Father will be happy for you, Samuel. You cannot believe otherwise. I know he is stern but he does love you, and wants the best for you. A home, a wife, even you have come around to the idea now," said Percival, with a satisfied smile that made Samuel wince.

He could not even deny it.

"He will be glad, Samuel. You cannot think that he

has ever understood your love of the sea to the exclusion of all else?"

"I suppose." Samuel was already counting the seconds until the charade could end. Just the idea of settling down into a home and living the domestic life with a dull plump wife and screaming children; it had always made his skin crawl, although Amelia...was far from dull and children...He shook off the spark of desire that rushed through him.

"Sam?" Percival said, sobering.

Samuel rolled the brandy around his glass and finally sighed. "She does not truly want to marry me, Percy," he said. He looked up at his brother. He had not thought that the fact would be so distressing until just this moment when speaking the words aloud. "She does not love me. She will break off the engagement as soon as she discovers the truth about her father's death."

Percival stared at him. "Whatever do you mean? The girl has just accepted your proposal. She has some fondness for you surely. We all heard..."

Samuel shook his head and looked into his glass. "Fondness, perhaps, but she will not marry me. She needs me to take her to London; to seek answers. That is all."

Percival scowled.

"No, Percy." Samuel said. "I do not fault her for it. She is afraid. Her father's death troubles her."

"I don't understand. I thought her father died in a carriage accident."

"She believes there was foul play." Samuel ran a hand

through his hair wondering when he began to agree with her. He realized he trusted her judgement. She was unlike any women he had met before; most were silly, generally lack-a-wit and tedious. Lady Amelia was none of those things.

"Do you believe there was foul play? Or is this just fancy?"

Samuel cupped his hands around his drink. "I did not at first. I thought it was just grief of a young girl trying to make sense of a senseless accident, but that was before she showed me her father's book."

Percy put down his glass. "What sort of book?"

"That's just it, Percy. She has a cypher book, like yours." Samuel looked over his drink at his brother. Percival looked startled.

"Mine?"

"Do not, Percy," Samuel said with an edge of anger. "I don't know what the secretiveness is that surrounds these books, but I have always been honest with you. Give me the same curtesy. I know you are trying to protect me in some misguided older brother fashion, but I will have none of it. You were poisoned. You could have died. Someone gave you that poison and I think it is likely to do with this secrecy. Do you have any idea who?"

Percy shook his head. "I don't."

"First your poisoning, and within a day," Samuel continued thoughtful. "Amelia's father met with his fatal accident. I convinced myself that it was mere coincidence, until I saw Amelia's book and realized you had the same."

"And you are worried?"

"Of course I am." Samuel stood and paced. "You must tell me. What is this business? Did you meet with the late Duke, Amelia's father at the ball? Is the mischance related? Are you and he somehow... involved in something?"

Percy sighed. "Something illegal? No."

"I would never think it. More likely, you were trying to deduce the nature of the cypher, and got in someone's way." Samuel stopped at the fireplace and picked up the poker, stirring the dead ash idly.

"You are too perceptive by half. I did indeed speak with the previous Duke of Ely."

Samuel turned to his brother. "And?" Samuel persisted.

"He told me little. We were going to meet the week next. There seems to be some sort of contraband involved. Obviously the culprits found out more about us than we knew of them. We do not even know who is involved."

"Lady Amelia said her father was agitated on the night before he died. She says he feared for his life and then, well, he was dead." Samuel laid the poker aside.

Percy sipped his wine and shrugged. "I suppose murders have been made for less than a dukedom."

"Yes, but why poison *you*?" Samuel sat again beside his brother.

"Indeed."

"And why the cyphers?"

Percival shook his head. "No one would kill for simple thievery, and a duke, yet. No. It makes no sense, Samuel."

"Criminals do not commit crimes due to need, nor sense, my brother, but I must agree. It would most likely be some acquaintance of the late Duke. Still, how is this related to the contraband and how did theft and contraband lead to murder?"

"Of a duke, no less."

"There must be something more involved and I am going to find out what." Samuel stood again in agitation.

"Father and I tried," Percival said. We found nothing circumspect, that is why I was looking into the cyphers, and your Lady Amelia..."

Samuel turned in anger. "And you and father did not discuss this with me?"

"I think he wanted to leave you out of it. Mother would never forgive him if something happened to you."

"Mother?" Samuel ran a hand through his hair and shook his head. "If it is smugglers of contraband I have connections on the docks, Percy not you. I can trace the latitude and longitude that Amelia uncovered. I should discover what transpired at those locations."

"She did so much?" Percy said surprised. "She solved the cypher. Well then, she is most prodigious."

"Yes," Samuel agreed, and then stood. "And yet, no one was ever more provoking," he said. "I shall get the book and return directly."

With the book and papers open before them, the brothers settled in for an evening of study.

Percival was shocked when he saw how much been accomplished by Lady Amelia. "It is helpful I'm sure, having the full cypher book instead of the waterlogged piece of rubbish I was using, but I am still surprised at how much Lady Amelia accomplished. She is really quite clever." Percival said with a sidelong look at his brother. "Now aren't you glad I coaxed you into going to the Livingston's Ball?"

"No! Yes. Well, only because had I not attended you would have stayed at the damned ball and probably died for politeness sake!"

"Yes, brother. I owe you my life."

"I didn't mean it like that. I only meant that—oh dash it!" Samuel said embarrassed. He poured a glass of brandy, downed it, and then poured another glass which he sipped. He held up the decanter for Percy.

Percy shook his head and raised his half empty glass. "No. I am done,"

"Does your stomach still trouble you?" Samuel asked as he sat with his drink.

"A bit, when I imbibe, but it is only a slight bother now, nothing to worry about. One can hardly survive poisoning and come out the other side completely unscathed. Without you I would not have survived at all," Percy said ruefully. "I have no room to complain."

"It's only because I couldn't bear to be earl when father passes," Samuel said shuddering.

Percy barked a short laugh.

Samuel brought his thoughts back to the issue at hand. "I suppose father is still investigating this," he said. "Blindly poking around the docks?"

"He is," Percival gave a shrug as if to say, it was Father. How was he to stop him?

"Father will be the next to meet an accident," Samuel

said dourly. He drank his brandy in stony silence. "What clues has the man found?" he asked at last.

"Very little," Percy said. "We suspected smuggling of course, but until recently, we were at a loss. Now, thanks to your Lady Amelia, and the cypher, we have locations to check. Perhaps they are meeting places or drop points. If they match with the actual contraband, well, so much the better."

"Yes," Samuel agreed. "We must write to Father."

Percy agreed.

"I am going to solve this. Amelia will not let it go at any rate."

"You would risk yourself for her?" Percy said. "To discover what happened to her father?"

"For her and for you, my brother."

After working for a while longer, Samuel frowned into his brandy glass. "I think we have solved all we can here," he said. "And the candles are guttering. We should take this up in the morning."

Percival agreed rubbing his eyes with the back of his hand. "I think we will find no more understanding here tonight. We will address it on the morrow."

"I wish it wasn't so, but Amelia is right. We will need to return to London."

"You don't mean to take her?"

"Of course not, but if I mean it or no, I think she will manage to follow. She is a spirited thing, unlike your little mouse. Speaking of, are you going to offer for her?"

"I don't want to be forward," Percival said.

Samuel broke into raucous laughter "Don't be an arse,

Percy" Samuel said, "Your little mouse is smitten. There is nothing to worry about."

"Do you truly think Lady Patience would have me?" Percival said, tugging his cravat lower down his neck to let more air in.

"Of course," said Samuel. "Do you not have eyes?"

"I am not ready to ask her. It is too soon. We hardly know each other and I think she is as frightened as I am."

"The little mouse seems to be frightened of everything." said Samuel "That is not the question to ask, Percy, not, is she frightened, but are you certain of her?"

"I am!" said Percival. "I am. But I am not like you. I cannot just rush into this without considering everything first, and of course she must meet Father before I go ahead with it. I am sure he will approve of her, but that is the proper way of things...ask our father; then speak to hers."

He did not say "and I am a gentleman and do things the proper way, unlike my brother" but Samuel heard the undertone and held back a snort. If he ever did fall in love with a woman and decided, against all better judgement, to truly marry her, he would not need anyone's permission. No one would be able to stop him.

"Are you so nervous about proposing to Lady Patience? You are sweating, Percy. Do not do that when the moment comes; no one wants to marry a frog."

"You are so helpful brother; why did I not think of that?" Percival said dryly. He dropped his head into his hands. "It's just the drink," he said. He looked up, a grin on his face, obviously more drunk than sick "It seems poisoning cures drunkenness."

Samuel laughed. "I don't know any man who would take the cure."

"Surely not by choice." Percy grimaced and pushed the last of his glass aside. "I am for bed," he said. "This business has made an old man of me."

Samuel scoffed, but finished off his brandy and also found his bed.

17

*T*he morning found Lady Amelia in the music room. She was an engaged woman now, she told herself. In the next moment she reminded herself that it was a lie. The ruse was only to give her a reason to go to London to find the truth of her father's death. Her fingers glided over the keys, and music filled her ears, drowning out her turbulent thoughts. The song of the sea was coming together in her mind, but the execution of it eluded her, much like the man who inspired it, she thought. Her fingers stuttered on the keys and she went back; playing the section again, perfecting it, polishing it. She played it a third time for clarity. It's almost there, she told herself. Almost.

"Beautiful," Samuel pronounced behind her.

She startled. "Thank you." She had not seen him there.

"I meant the woman as well as the music," he said.

"Then my thanks are doubled," she replied.

"Breakfast will be served shortly," he said. "Will you walk with me?"

"Certainly." She stood smoothing her dress.

"I have ordered tea in the garden while we wait to break our fast," he said. "The morning is still and clear, if a bit brisk."

"Is that the sort of morning you enjoy on your ship?" she asked.

"I do," he said as they sat in the garden and watched the huge golden sun hover just above the horizon. It was a day that promised warmth and sun, but the morning was still cool.

Amelia sipped her tea. It was prepared as she liked it with a bit of honey and lots of cream and the warmth of it filled her. She closed her eyes in appreciation, and when she opened her eyes, Samuel was smiling at her. It was a disconcerting feeling. He was her fiancé now. Why did she feel so tongue-tied, when she had never had that problem before? She shook off the lethargy and asked when they would be returning to London. They finished their tea and then walked around the immaculate garden as they talked.

Samuel convinced Amelia that she, Patience and Aunt Ebba should return to the country house and pack for London properly. Although she wanted to hurry, she knew he was right when he said that haste would be foolhardy.

"In making plans for our London excursion," Samuel said. "It occurred to me that undo haste would call attention to us and foster gossip. Better for you ladies to finish your visit, leave here as planned, then all of you back to your country house and on to London after a few days respite. This will give us time to prepare, and you can pack for London at your leisure. Deportment will stop the gossip."

"Nothing will stop the gossip," Amelia said. "However, I will write the announcement to the Times…" She hesitated. "Oh, no," she said. "You would have to first ask my father…" the wrenching pain that passed through her at the memory of his death caused her to catch her breath. "… my uncle, I mean" Amelia whispered. Her face turned pale as ice. She sank down on a garden bench. "This will not do."

"So we can't let London know via the Times?" Samuel asked. "The whole point of this…engagement is to let London know so that you will have some freedom of movement."

Amelia was silent, tapping a slippered foot on the garden walk. "But London does not need to know via the Times," Amelia said thoughtfully. "I will write to Charity…no. She is vexed with me. I will have Patience write to Charity and tell her that you have asked me to marry, and plan to call upon the duke when you come into London to ask his leave. Then the news of our imminent engagement will precede us."

"Surely this will not be as efficient as the Times," Samuel said.

"Oh, Samuel," she said pityingly. "You know nothing of gossip. Charity will be much more effective."

By now, the house was stirring and the smell of cooking sausages invaded the garden walk. Samuel tucked Amelia's hand on his arm and she allowed him to escort her to breakfast with the others.

THE REMAINDER of the week flew by, Amelia and Samuel catching moments here and there, but he did not kiss her again. She found herself feeling the loss. Patience and Percival, on the other hand, had been seen strolling hand in hand in the garden several times, and once Patience's bonnet was slightly askew when she returned from a walk. Aunt Ebba was beaming and planning both of their weddings with opulent enthusiasm. Amelia felt disgraceful to be deceiving her. She caught Samuel's eye on her then, and looked pointedly away.

Still Amelia found herself relaxing, she enjoyed mornings in the music room with Samuel and her piano and evenings with Samuel and his brother, at first she had thought Lord Beresford somewhat diffident, but apparently his unwillingness to engage in conversation had just been a response of his illness. She had now found that Percival had a wry wit, and was a perfect foil for his brash brother. She laughed at their antics and envied their comradery, especially now that she had no parents as well as no siblings. When she bemoaned the lack to her friend, Patience had comforted her saying, "You have a sister in me."

"And of course, I am your brother," Percival had added.

Patience looked up sharply then, and Percival added in explanation, "As Lady Amelia is marrying my brother."

For just a moment Patience looked glum but then, a little quirk in Percival's smile had her smiling again.

THE SUN ROSE BRIGHTLY and birds were singing on the morning the three women were to leave Stanherd Residence for Amelia's own country home. Or rather her Uncle Declan's now, Amelia thought with a scowl. It was a perfect day for travel and although she felt some sadness at her departure, Amelia was excited to finally be able to pursue answers regarding her father's death. It was clear, however, that Samuel was going to do his best to keep her inquiries at bay. She smiled. He did not know her well. She was used to getting her own way, and did not intend to cease now.

At breakfast they spoke of the possible events in London which Percival and Patience might attend. Aunt Ebba spoke to Amelia about announcing the wedding while still in mourning and sending a letter to her uncle in London in advance of their arrival when Samuel entered with the statement that he had directed the servants to load the carriage and all should be ready to go after breakfast.

Patience and Amelia shared a look over their teacups.

"What is it?" Samuel asked.

"Aunt Ebba likes to attend the packing," Patience said.

"I do not like it," Aunt Ebba said. "But it is a necessary burden I must bear."

After breakfast, the carriage was prepared in accordance with Aunt Ebba's overwhelming need to control every piece of luggage, so much so that Amelia knew if her aunt had been a man, she would have just dismissed the servants and shouldered their trunks into the carriage herself.

Percival and Patience had fled to the garden.

Once everything had been wedged, pushed and pulled into its proper place, Aunt Ebba turned to Samuel, "I do hope it is no trouble to escort us home," she said, as if that would make any difference at all, now that the carriage was full to the hilt.

"Of course not," Samuel said helping the ladies into the carriage. "It is my pleasure."

Conversation in the carriage was of Amelia and Samuel's upcoming nuptials. Aunt Ebba had begun devising the guest list of her side of the family and even had a long list from Amelia's father's side. "Of course, your uncle will give you away," she said.

Amelia shuddered at the thought.

"When you speak to him, Commander Beresford, to ask for her hand, do be on your best behavior." Aunt Ebba smoothed her gloves as she spoke. "He has little sense of humor and can be a tedious man, but he is, nonetheless, the duke now.

Amelia frowned at her Aunt. "Do not glower so," she said to her niece and addressed her along with Samuel. "If the duke gets it in his mind that you have somehow wronged him, he could vex you past bearing.

"Why would he think we wronged him?" Amelia asked.

Aunt Ebba waved a gloved hand. "He is simply, not the most obliging of men. He tends to find fault where there is none." Both Amelia and Samuel were largely silent on the topic then, answering only direct inquiries, while Patience punctuated Aunt Ebba's long expositions on the topic of weddings in general, and theirs specifically.

"With you in mourning," Aunt Ebba said, "We will have to wait at least until Christmas, or just after, and the weather is likely to be poor as we get into January. Even then, you will be out of black, but will not have a true choice of colors, nor design, Amelia. I'm thinking spring. What are your thoughts? Commander?"

They answered together.

"Wait until spring," Amelia said.

"I like Christmas," Samuel said.

They looked at one another tongue-tied and then Amelia looked at her hands, fiddling with her gloved fingers. Samuel looked out the window.

Both felt they could not get to Amelia's home soon enough, but Percival and Patience picked up the conversation with discussions of what flowers were already in bloom and what she might plant in her garden and what would grow best in London.

Amelia had not known of Lord Beresford's interest in gardening, or even in Samuel's occasional addition to the conversation. Their mother was quite the gardener, and had kept her sons busy with growing things when the boys were youngsters. She was gifted with a mental picture of little boys side by side digging in the dirt and pulling weeds. If young Samuel brushed his hair back as he was so often want to do, he no doubt would have had a streak of dirt from his nose to his ear. Considering the tall naval man in front of her today, thinking of him tending flowers as a boy gave her a warm feeling and she smiled in spite of herself. Little surprises like that made her realize how little she really knew about him. Still the talk of gardening was a welcome distraction from wedding plans that would never come to pass. She had not expected this lie to be so hard; it seemed every other word was a deception.

THEY ARRIVED in the early evening and had dinner with her uncle's people serving. She remembered then that he had replaced the estate's servants. There was not a familiar face among them and Amelia immediately felt less at home than she had at the Beresford's.

"Why don't you play the piano for us," Samuel had suggested after dinner. "Have you finished the piece you are working on?"

"No," she said blushing, embarrassed that her ode to the sea had originally been inspired by him.

"Well. No matter. I love hearing you play," he said, which drew a knowing smile shared between Patience and Percival. The little party gathered their drinks and removed to the music room, where Amelia found her piano. She stared at it unwilling to believe what she was seeing.

She felt bereft. Her piano was covered with a great canvas clothe, and when she asked a footman to remove it, he had told her that the duke had ordered it so.

Amelia just stared at him, about ready to cry. "But I wish to play my piano," Amelia said.

"Pardon M'lady," the footman had said. "But the piano is the duke's and he has ordered it prepared for storage, or perhaps sale. I am not privy to his plans."

"Sale!" Amelia thought she would be sick. This was *her piano*, the one she learned on, it was older than the tall cabinet one her father had bought for her back in the London house. It was at this piano she had first put her fingers to the keys, when her young hands had been too small to reach all the notes and her feet dangled off the bench, too short to reach floor. She couldn't breathe. This could not be happening. Her fingers itched to play, or hit something. She wanted to scream.

"Amelia," Aunt Ebba had soothed. "Amelia, it's alright."

"No. It's not," she said tears brimming.

Samuel pushed past the footman and moved to remove the heavy canvas, but the footman stopped him. "I'm sorry, sir," he said, "Please, won't you go back to the drawing room?"

"No, dammit," Samuel said and there was a tense moment when Amelia thought that Samuel might actually hit the footman, but Percival interrupted.

"We will return to the drawing room," he said to the footman.

Patience, always believing the best of everyone said, "Perhaps your uncle will give you the piano for a wedding present. You don't know...."

He is a horrid man, Amelia thought. I hate him. How

could he possibly be my father's brother? How could my father die, and this man still live?

"Just because it is covered does not mean it is gone." Aunt Ebba said. "In any case, we are for London soon, and there is your marriage to look forward to...."

Amelia nearly burst into tears. Her upcoming wedding was a sham. Her father was gone, and she had been banished to the country at the whim of her horrid uncle. Now he would take her music as well. She clenched her hands into fists. She would not cry. She would see this despicable man made low for what he had done. She would, but first, she had to get control of herself. "Excuse me," she said softly. She got to her feet and hurried from the room.

Amelia had gone to her father's study then, with Aunt Ebba following murmuring apologies to their guests and condolences to her niece. Amelia thought she would just sit and try to regain her self-possession where she felt most close to her father. The room still held his scent; it would settle her. She hoped it could give her just a moment of peace where she could remember her father as he once was and regain her composure.

Again the footman followed. This time he caught her at the door and said, "I'm sorry, Lady Atherton. The duke has ordered several rooms off limits. This is one of them."

"Now, see here," Samuel began to berate the man at her elbow, and she took the opportunity to push past them both and open the door.

When Amelia looked into the study, she stopped in shock. Everything had been moved. Her father's life and hers packed up in crates and boxes. Her eyes flew to the desk where she had found the mysterious cypher book. It was ransacked; every drawer emptied. In her mute astonishment a single dreadful thought broke through her clouded mind: her uncle had searched for the book. She couldn't breathe. She felt suddenly dizzy, the room spinning. And for the first time in her life, Amelia fainted.

18
――――

*A*melia awoke in her bed. She wondered if it was the awful footman who had carried her there. Surely not. Perhaps Samuel had carried her, and she did not even know it. That thought brought a blush to her skin and a smile to her lips. She suddenly wanted to see him, to hear his voice talk about their plans...then she remembered their plans were all a pretense. But still, she told herself, it would be good to be busy. She must do something.

At breakfast, Samuel and Percy spoke briefly of the London plans and when Samuel asked if she was feeling well, indicating her fainting spell last night, Amelia discretely noted with her eyes that all of the servants were of course, her uncle's. Gone was the comfort of her childhood home, replaced with a wary disquiet. The sooner she could leave this house the better.

Samuel grimaced; understanding her instantly. "My

brother and I can return to Standherd and be back on the morrow to escort you to London," He said tightly.

"Oh, goodness, we cannot be repacked for Town so quickly," Aunt Ebba replied.

"When would you like us to return?" Percival asked.

"In other words, how quickly might you be able?" Patience explained to Aunt Ebba.

"Oh, at least a week," Aunt Ebba said.

"I will help Auntie," Amelia said. "We can be ready in two days."

"Four," Aunt Ebba countered.

"Auntie, your trucks are packed," Amelia pointed out.

"And yours are not," Aunt Ebba said. "Do you want to move to London or do you want to have to come back for more of your belongings in the next few weeks. It is clear to me that your uncle doesn't want you here."

Amelia bit her lip. "I have nowhere else to go."

"Nonsense," Aunt Ebba said. "You are coming to London with me, and soon enough you will have your own house." She sent a big smile Samuel's way and patted Amelia's hand.

"You are always welcome at my home, Amelia," Patience said. "Father would not mind an extended visit and my mother would love to see you again."

"Lady Amelia," Percival said. "My father recently gave my brother and I an apartment in London to use while he was at Lords. It is at your disposal while you are in Town. After all it belongs to my brother as well as to me."

"I will make my own way," Samuel said tightly to Percival, "But Amelia and I should indeed search for a townhouse while we are in London."

"Samuel," Percy began, but Samuel interrupted him, turning to the women. "It is decided then; we will return four days hence."

OUTSIDE IN THE MORNING, while the brothers were taking their leave, Amelia and Samuel had only a brief moment to talk and even then they were cautious of the servants. "I am so glad I left the cypher book at Standherd with you." Amelia told him. "I'm afraid of my uncle; I know he is involved now. Did you see my father's study?"

"I saw it, but what about it upset you so?" Samuel asked.

"It was searched," Amelia said. "He or his servants were looking for the book."

"You can't know that," Samuel began trying to soothe her, but she gave him an incredulous look. "Do you think me a ninny?"

"No, of course not, I think you are probably right, but nothing can come of worrying. We will solve this mystery together." Samuel said as he caught her hand. But you won't be here, she thought. She wished she was not wearing gloves. She wanted to feel the skin of him. She wanted him to kiss her again, but of course he did not. There was no privacy in her uncle's home.

She grasped his other hand and leaned close. It was terribly forward, but they were engaged and she didn't want him to go. "Samuel, he knows," she whispered.

He gripped her hands tightly. "He cannot know. He can only suspect, and he is not here. He is in London."

"But if he is the one...we announced our engagement. London will know by now, and if he wanted to keep your brother and my father apart..." she took a shaky breath. "We have just told him *we are together*."

Samuel embraced her, ignoring the scandalized looks of uncle's servants. He kissed her forehead and whispered against it. "Four days. I will return for you in four days."

She watched as Samuel and Percival rode away, feeling more bereft by the minute. She stood, eyes surveying Samuel's retreating form and did not turn to go back inside the manor until the brothers were well out of sight.

THE NEXT FEW days were a flurry of unpacking and repacking. Aunt Ebba was in a state. Amelia did not know she had so much to move. Each day she tried to spend just a few minutes in the music room. The piano was covered with canvas, but she could sit in her father's chair and remember him. It calmed her a bit. At least the furniture had not been moved. The footman who had been so insolent before was quite helpful with her packing, and Amelia was glad she no longer had the book with her. The footman let her sit in the music room and let her take her tea there. She wondered if her belongings were being searched while she rested here, but it didn't matter. She no longer had anything to find. She used the time to say good bye to her father, and promise him that she would find out the truth.

SAMUEL AND PERCY planned the London trip with care. They decided that Percy would take both books and all of the relevant papers and ride for London that very night. It was the best way to keep his health a secret, but riding at night always had some risk.

Samuel wrote a letter to his father, and Percy took it. "I will speak to him," Percival said. "Show him what you and Amelia have made of the cyphers."

"We will be in London in four days," he reminded Percy. "As early as we can... You need to find the contraband before that. Once we get there, I expect we'll be in the devil's own scrape. I don't expect the duke to leave me and Amelia in peace and I will have to speak with him directly."

"I know," Percy said.

"Don't end in a ditch somewhere, traveling in the dark," Samuel said.

"Now, you sound like mother," Percival joked.

Samuel scoffed. "We are counting on you," he said. "And I don't want to be the bloody earl."

Percival grinned. "Aye, *Sir*," he teased.

"Don't get cheeky," Samuel said.

"I know," Percy said sobering. "These people are serious. I was poisoned, remember." Percival gripped his brother's shoulder. "I don't like you being in danger either, Sam. You will have a target on your back once you get to Town."

"They aren't going to poison me, or run me down with a carriage."

"No. You are more likely to get a knife in your back."

"That is a chance you take on the docks," Samuel said. "It's never totally safe, and it would be normal for me to go there, Percy. Besides, I want someone to protect us when we get to London, someone to protect Amelia." If I can't, was implied in his words.

"Nonetheless," Percival replied. "Be careful."

"I will," Samuel said pushing the house seal into the wax of the second letter and handing it to Percy. "This one is for mother," Samuel said. "I told her to meet us in London, and that you will be staying with her for secrecy. She is probably beside herself if she has heard the rumors of your demise. I told her only you were ill, no details."

Percy chuckled and placed the letters in the leather satchel. "She's still in Bath," Percival predicted. "I'll post the letter when I get to Town."

"What about Lady Patience? Should I give her any word?" Samuel asked as they walked together to the stable.

"I will speak to her once she arrives in London," Percival promised.

Samuel said nothing, but looked up at the moon. It was a bright half circle that would keep the road at least partially lit. The groom brought out Percy's horse, all tacked and ready to go. He had been riding the mount since he was a lad, and the beast was a sensible thing. Percival tightened the straps of the satchel and checked the girth. The groom gave him a leg up. There was nothing else to do.

"Godspeed," Samuel said finally.

"And you brother."

Percy touched the horse with his heels and it moved into a steady trot. Within moments it was lost to the night.

Samuel watched his brother go, thinking he would have the longest four days of his life in front of him. He was not made for stillness.

SAMUEL WAS up at the break of dawn and after swallowing a cold breakfast which could have been procured on a ship, he made his way to Aunt Ebba's country home to escort the women to London. He pushed the horses a little harder than he should have, considering the load they would have to pull to London, but he was anxious to assure himself that Amelia was well.

"Where is Lord Beresford?" Patience asked, concerned. "Is he well? I thought he was joining us."

"He is fine," Samuel assured her. "He had some business to attend to. My mother is also returning to London. Rest assured he will call on you at his earliest convenience."

Patience beamed.

Eventually, everything was packed and ready to go. Samuel had hoped to be on their way at least an hour ago, and was agitated when they finally got moving. He had also hoped to be able to talk freely with Amelia, but that too was frustrated by the presence of the other two women. He didn't want to worry them with talk of cypher books and murder, but after mulling it over for the last three and a half days he was edgy himself.

The conversation in the carriage revolved around which events were still to come in the London Season, and which of those events Amelia could in good taste attend. Aunt Ebba fussed over which of Amelia's evening gowns could be made suitable for mourning attire or at least half mourning; perhaps some Aunt Ebba's own could be refitted. Aunt Ebba had expected Amelia to be overjoyed with the conversation, but she seemed tense. Samuel reached out, his fingertips touching her cheek. She leaned against his touch for a moment; then shook his hand away.

"Are you not excited to go back to London?" Aunt Ebba asked.

"Of course," she said automatically, but her heart was not wholly convinced. Of course it would normally be wonderful to be in London, but she was not ready to return to town, to face everyone there, to see the places she used to frequent, places where she, the queen of the ball, would no longer reign; but for her father, she would endure. For her father, she could even face Uncle Declan.

The more Aunt Ebba chattered on about wedding plans, the more reticent she became. Samuel tried to engage Lady Patience about Percival, but she blushed and stuttered. Eventually conversation dwindled and Amelia began to nod off. She was trying so hard to sit straight and proper, but eventually she lost the battle.

Samuel's jaw ached. He had been gritting his teeth through the last hour of the carriage ride. Both Aunt Ebba and Lady Patience had nodded off across from him.

He would have used this time to talk to Amelia, but she had fallen asleep too. He supposed, like himself, she was not getting much sleep lately. This would not have been a problem, but her head had lolled over onto his shoulder after a particularly bumpy section of road. Now he had to stay as still, lest he wake her.

He had wrapped his arm around Amelia to keep her from falling and now, his arm was asleep, a mass of tingling, but in sleep, her face had softened. It was breathtaking and proud, worthy of a figurehead. Worst of all, or perhaps best of all, one of her sleeves had fallen down her shoulder, exposing an expanse of cream-colored skin, completely unblemished. It was likely the shoulder had never felt another man's touch, which filled Samuel with an intense desire to touch it.

He sighed. Even asleep, the woman could drive him mad.

Once at Aunt Ebba's London townhouse, he saw the ladies settled.

"Is your husband in town?" he asked Aunt Ebba, and she assured him that he was. It gave Samuel some measure of comfort that the women would not be alone.

He spoke briefly with Amelia to reassure her and then bid her good night with a promise that he would arrive in the morning to put on a show of looking for houses. They would have time to talk more in the carriage. He would have loved to stay and simply spend the evening with her, but it was imperative that he go to the docks tonight. Already too much time had passed.

19

The London port on the Thames was still busy when Samuel arrived which was just as he planned. He made himself well seen along the boardwalk, greeting some of the other officers he knew in passing from other ships. He made himself very visible to draw out any of the men who may be in the employ of the duke. He did not see any of Percy's men searching the docks, but he supposed that was a good thing.

The salt air was as familiar as his own breath, as he worked his way around the docks. He had no specific destination, but rather, he wanted to seem like he was surveying the whole of the area. In a very brief period of time, he actually began to relax. The smell of fish, from the whale blubber being rendered and fishermen's sale huts filled his nose as the wind shifted along the docks. The shouts of sailors reminded him of home. He did not belong in a rich manse. He belonged here. Here he did not need to watch his step or his words. Here he could be himself. He was not an earl's son. He was simply Commander Beresford.

Still, family was family, and Percy needed him, and now there was the Lady Amelia Atherton to consider... and the other Amelia he loved just as well, his fine ship. One day she would be truly his. He looked up at his proud ship in the harbor.

He could not help but look for something amiss, even though that was not his intent here tonight. There were several possibilities in his mind as to the cause of the trouble and none would bode well for Lady Amelia. It bothered him that his brother had any business with the illegal activity. He felt the danger as a chill creeping up the back of his neck. He had no intension of involving a lady in the affair, especially not his lady. He shook his head. When had he begun to think of the irascible Lady Amelia as his? Perhaps when she suggested they should pretend to be betrothed. He smiled wryly thinking of the flush of heat in her kiss before she had remembered herself.

He attempted to bring his mind back to the matter at hand. The cypher was not specific, but he could surmise that the contraband, whatever it was, would be in one of the warehouses along the West India Docks. Was it munitions? With the threat of war still looming that was a possibility, or maybe some other valuables. Most items he could think of might entice a sailor, but not a duke, and none of them would be worth killing a man over, especially not a member of the Peerage.

He, or rather Percy and the guard, should be able to locate the cargo, since ships were often caught in a kind of maritime traffic jam for weeks on end. The warehouses were paramount to allow ships to discharge their goods and move on, but why the secrecy and code books? Why murder? There was only one reason he could think of. The cargo at that warehouse could only be something that by its very possession was a risk of life and limb.

He made himself alert to any unusual activity on the waterfront, but saw none. The rhythmic clop clop of the ships rolling to the waves against the docks was soothing. The ships docked were varied, but that was nothing out of the ordinary. Seamen and wenches populated the boardwalk, talking in loud rough voices. Some were already drunk.

He walked towards the cluster of establishments where he knew he could find members of his own crew and perhaps even friends.

"Carlton! White!" Samuel exclaimed as he saw a few of the men from his ship. He knew them marginally well, but as a Commander, did not generally mingle with them. They were Danny Carlton and George White, both young petty officers.

The two men paused a bit uncomfortably, came to attention but did not salute as neither was in uniform, and Samuel was also in civvies. "Commander," they addressed him. He was not used to socializing with the crew, but he would feel better with men he knew at his back.

"Commander," Danny Carlton said politely.

Another seaman from his ship caught up to them, patting White on the back and urging him to come have a drink. He saw Commander Beresford and snapped to attention. It took Samuel a moment to place the man as, Jerry Walter. "We have missed you, Commander," he said.

"My brother has been ill," Samuel replied. "And I've had family business."

"You aren't going to leave us for Lords now are you, Sir?" Carlton asked. "We have heard rumors..." Carlton hesitated "Rumors that your brother is bad off."

"Or dead," George White added tastelessly. "You may be the heir."

"We're all sorry to hear..." Jerry Walters broke in.

Samuel's jaw tightened. He didn't like that the rumors were that his brother was near death, or dead, but on the other hand, that particular rumor was planned to protect Percy and to keep his presence in London a secret; at least for a time.

"...or that you may become a tenant for life," Carlton grinned widely. "Who's the lucky lady?"

"When's the nuptials?" Walters asked.

"News travels fast," Sam noted. He had doubted Amelia's friend Charity would do as well as the Times with their engagement announcement. Obviously, he was wrong.

"And Danny here can't even read," George White joked, poking his friend, the presence of alcohol making him more jovial than usual.

"We are on the cut," Danny Carlton explained gesturing to the pub. "Might we toast your lady, Commander?"

"Yes, thank you. I think I will have a drink with you," Samuel said.

"The Commander'd never leave us for his father,"

George White said, "but I guess, maybe for a woman." They all laughed.

"I'd bet gold on that," Danny Carlton said.

"You don't have any gold," Samuel joked back, putting the men at ease. "I know your salaries; but speaking of gold. I do have a favor to ask, and it may include a spot of coin."

"You know we are always up for a bit of work, Commander," Carlton said.

"This is not official," Samuel warned.

George White shrugged. "Damned low water for me. I'm in for some blunt."

"Leave it to us, Commander," Danny Carton said.

"Good then. I'll stop back on the morrow," Samuel said.

"No, have that drink with us," White urged.

"Are you buying?" Walters asked with a grin.

"No. You are," Carlton said with a teasing laugh.

White shoved him into the pub.

"I'm buying," Samuel said as he followed the three men into the establishment where they proceeded to toast, Samuel's fiancée, the beautiful Lady Amelia Atherton. After dipping rather deep, Samuel began to wax poetic about her beauty himself: toasting her eyes and her lips, and her hair. Before the conversation became too bawdy, he told them of her music, lamenting that his reason must have been swallowed in her song. Some of the men laughed. Others began singing.

"'Tis well then, you are going to marry the girl," Danny Carlton said, as he and Samuel left the pub. Samuel agreed, some sense coming back to him as the cool sea air hit his face. Somehow Jerry Walter got Samuel on his horse and sent him on his way with the promise that the seamen would join his employ for as long as he needed them and they were in port. Their willingness to help put his mind at rest.

He did not tell them, that his engagement was only a ruse. He held that particular pain, like a barnacle on his own heart, and instead reminded Carlton that he would meet them early on the morrow.

Samuel arrived home sometime near dawn mainly due to the fact that his horse had a good sense of direction. The drink had made him maudlin and as he fell into bed for a few hours rest, he could think of nothing but Amelia, and the fact that she was not truly his.

20

――――――

*A*melia was waiting. Samuel's note had explicitly stated he would arrive at nine in the morning, and so she had risen early and broken her fast. It was closer to ten now and he was nowhere in sight. At fifteen minutes past the hour she had gone back to sit at the window. She was nearly finished composing her song for the sea; Samuel's song. The tune ran through her head, but without a piano here at Aunt Ebba's, she could not finish it. The ending eluded her. Should it be uplifting, and end with a happier note, or carry the tragic, adventurous feeling of the song to the very end? When she had frustrated herself long enough, she had ordered another cup of tea. Still, she waited. After thirty-five minutes had passed with no Samuel, she was beginning to think he had forgotten about her, and that was infuriating, as she thought of him at least every other moment for reasons unknown to her. He was as intriguing as he was irritating.

Finally at quarter past ten, she heard the crunch of wheels on the stone drive and the shuffling leather of the horses in their harness. She rose, taking her time. It would be good to make *him* wait now. She planned to do just that, but a moment later the front door burst open and Commander Samuel Beresford was striding into the room.

"Are you ready? Good, come along. We must hurry," he said, waving his hand at her as if she were a dog. Did he think she would answer to a wave and a whistle?

"I beg your pardon," Amelia said balking. "I have been waiting for you for over an hour and now you tell me to make haste? You presume too much."

"What presumption?" he asked. "I have been put to a vast deal of inconvenience already this morning," Samuel said.

"You? You?" Amelia sputtered. "I had breakfast at eight, so as not to inconvenience you."

"And no doubt you were awake at six and at your piano."

"Aunt Ebba has no piano," she spat.

"Oh," he said instantly contrite. "That would have made the wait more tedious. I would as soon, you stayed safely at home," he said softly, "But I expect you will have none of it. Come along then. Shall we be off?"

Amelia glared at him. "I am reconsidering it now," she said. "Will you be civil, or is this the sort of behavior I can expect?"

Samuel closed his eyes, took a breath, and held out an arm to Amelia. When she hesitated he said, "I am sorry. I had a... difficult morning."

"What happened, perchance?" she asked.

"I do not propose to bother you with the matter," he said. "I will behave myself. Please, come with me?"

Though she knew the apology was as much of an act as his pretending to be betrothed to her, it still melted away her anger. She did not accept his arm, however, and stalked past him out the open front door and right into the carriage, leaving him to follow like a footman.

The actual footman was a young man she didn't know. He stood nervously as they approached, looking from one to the other.

Samuel hurried to catch up. "You are a most provoking woman," he said.

"And you are a vain and thoughtless man," Amelia retorted. "Now, what is it you have learned?" She was anxious to find any further clue to the books and cyphers.

"Very little," he said. "We have only just arrived in London."

Her breath caught for just a moment, and then she turned on the street and said. "We were supposed to be finding out the truth to this business. At any time my uncle could decide I must come home. We cannot dally."

"I am aware," he said.

"Must I do everything myself?" she asked.

He laid a hand on her gloved one, aware that she was as tense as he was, perhaps more so with the threat of her uncle over her head. He leaned close and said, "I told you. It is not safe. I would not take you any further if..."

This was something she could be angry about. She jerked away from him. "I am the one who found the rest of the cypher. Without me you would have been stuck fast," she hissed under her breath.

"Hush," he said softly taking her arm and pulling her close so he could whisper in her ear. "Gossips are everywhere on London streets. Would you shout at me like a common fish wife?"

The footman helped her into the carriage a little awkwardly and Samuel followed.

"Thank you Carlton," Samuel said as he sat down beside her, tapping the roof of the carriage to signal the driver onward. The driver did not at once move, and Samuel tapped again a bit harder.

"Remember," he said to her, "We are a young betrothed couple, and if we are to have people believe it is a love match, you must stop looking daggers at me. What is wrong?"

"You were late," she said. Lady Amelia Atherton had never in her life waited upon a suitor. They waited upon her: all of them. It irked her pride that he did not. Of course he wasn't really a suitor.

"It was unavoidable," Samuel said without explanation.

She lifted her chin, and pasted an utterly insincere smile on her face. It was just the sort of bored haughty look she had bestowed on her other suitors when he had interrupted them at the ball. It felt like a kick in the gut.

Her coolness was grating on him, and more than anything, he wanted to see her smile again. More than that, too much danger was following them for them to be at odds. He directed the driver to the first house of the day.

"You could have sat across from me," Amelia groused, trying to edge away from him. She did not try too hard, because his arm was warm against her side and she could smell the soap he had used that morning. His face was clean-shaven and his hair was shining and dark, combed back neatly as she had requested. He had clearly made an effort, which was a surprise.

"But we are betrothed," said Samuel, looking over at her. "We can be intimate now."

"We can be no such thing," said Amelia. "We are not truly betrothed and even if we were, decency is still required of us. You are just being deliberately vulgar to upset me, I know it. Why do you say such things?"

"To see you blush," said Samuel, simply.

Amelia did not reply but sat in stony silence. When the carriage stopped, the footman Carlton, opened the door to hand them out. She did not recognize the street.

"I thought we were going to the docks," she said.

"No," he said simply. "We have to look at townhouses while we are out, just so we have something to talk about when we return to your Aunt's house," said Samuel. "She would think it odd if we were only gone a few short hours, or if we had nothing to say when we returned."

Amelia nodded suddenly uncomfortable. Actually looking at houses together felt entirely too intimate. She felt him watching her assessing her reaction. She fixed her eyes on the townhouse. There were steps up through an archway to the front door, which had stained glass window above it. A quaint balcony with an iron railing graced the second floor. It was not as garish as Charity's father's townhouse, but not as plain as Aunt Ebba's and

Uncle Edward's. It was smaller than Aunt Ebba's, but it did have a certain charm. It was on a popular street, and Patience's father's was not far from here which would be convenient for visiting. It was all a ruse, she reminded herself

"It is quaint," she said.

"A beauty," he said his eyes locked on her and she gave him her coolest stare. Then he gestured to the house. "Shall we go inside? What do you think?"

She narrowed her eyes. "Think?" she said.

"Yes. Would you like to live here? I know it is not large, but I think it is quite cozy." Samuel continued, telling her about the house, and she suddenly wanted to bolt. Thoughts tumbled over one another as she thought of coming home to this house...with him. No. She would not even think such things. He was a common seaman. She was Lady Amelia Atherton. She would not.

"I think not," she said tersely. She turned to get back into the carriage and the footman floundered to help her given her sudden change of direction. What should have been done in the cool morning hours was now commencing at midday. The sun was beaming down and the carriage was warm and humid. She snapped out her fan and began waving it vigorously in effort to cool herself.

The utter domesticity of the task was causing her some distress. Samuel, as usual seemed unaffected. When she got back into the carriage, she put down the fan and tugged at the ties of her bonnet, putting her fingers between her chin and the ribbons to loosen it.

Tugging, she realized she had put it into a knot. She struggled with it under her chin where she could not see it. Suddenly it felt very close in the carriage with Samuel beside her.

"I pity the woman who does marry you, Commander Beresford," she said. "You take nothing seriously. Let us remember that this trip is not to frolic around London looking at houses; it is to find proof of my father's murder," Amelia replied, turning her head away from him and staring out the window at the passing scene while she continued to fret with her ribbons.

Once she cleared her father's name and found out what had caused his demise, she could go back to the life she loved; to the life of men buzzing around her like bees. She could choose any of them. Her fingers stilled on the ribbons as she thought, And which would be the equal of Commander Samuel Beresford? Who would spar with her instead of running after her like a milksop, begging for crumbs? Who would excite her and fill her thoughts? Who would she find so enjoyable to be with? Who would kiss her like... She shoved that dangerous thought away.

"I take plenty of things seriously," Samuel was saying, "But this is a ruse, a game, and I am doing it for entertainment, not for profit. Therefore, I will treat it accordingly."

"And me, as well?" She began to work again with the ribbon. It was nigh and truly stuck now.

"What?"

"You will treat me as a part of this game?" said Amelia, spinning around to look at him.

"Well," said Samuel, one side of his mouth lifting into a smile. "Yes. You are a part of the game. A bit of fun."

She started to turn yanking viciously at the hat when his warm hand covered hers, stilling her frantic movement at the ribbons. His fingers found the ribbon at her throat, with careful patience picked at the knot until it was untied. Then he tugged her bonnet completely off and tossed it on the seat beside them.

"Sir!" she said.

His face was so close to hers she could see the darkening of his eyes, smell the scent of his cologne. But instead of kissing her, he pressed his lips against the top of her head, inhaling the sweet floral scent of her hair.

"I have never understood why women insist on wearing extravagant head pieces that cover up one of their most attractive features," he said.

"Excuse me, Commander Beresford, that is an expensive hat that you have just tossed off! My hair must be a mess beneath it," Amelia continued, bringing her hand up to smooth the strands down. "Unbelievable," said Amelia, shaking her head. "Are you going to pretend that our... encounters had no real effect on you? That it was just a part of the ruse? For what purpose? No one was present, but you and I."

"Pray tell. Which encounter are you speaking of?" he asked thinking of the several stolen kisses they had shared.

"Oh you are a cad," she snapped, swatting him with her fan.

He snatched at the fan, catching it mid-swing, with

lightening quick reflexes, his hand was warm, his face inches from her own. Her eyes were wide and her lips parted, startled or in anticipation, he was not sure. "Do you not think kissing is fun. Oh, you definitely need a reminder," he said.

"Yes," she whispered, and then almost as if she realized what she had said, she scooted as far from him as she could, wedging herself in the corner of the coach. If he kissed her here, in the enclosed carriage, she was not sure she would keep her composure. "I do not believe you. Not for a second."

"The lady has moved," he said softly. "I think she is not as unaffected by my kisses as she would have me believe."

Amelia looked at him wide eyed. How was it that he knew her so well? "I?" she said. "You are the one who walked from the music room." He was mocking her. She had to remember this was only a ruse. "You are laughing at me now."

"Never, Lady Amelia. I would never laugh at you. You are elegance and passion in equal measure, surely you do not think me one to pass up such a ripe opportunity, to kiss a beautiful woman," he said his lips so close to hers she could almost taste them, and yet he did not kiss her.

He had called her beautiful, and elegant, and passionate. Her heart did a little flip flop, and kept racing wildly. But it was a ruse. He had never truly offered for her. It was just a lark. "Pray do not be so provoking," she said jutting her chin out and daring him to challenge her.

"How so?"

"Our encounters meant nothing to you," She said.

"Whatever gave you that idea?" he asked.

"You are so flippant," she said.

"You are the one who could not keep your mind on the kiss...spouting off about books and cyphers."

"Oh, what folly has entered my mind? You were only teasing me."

"A folly we share," he said.

"I only wished to speak of the books...." She started to pull away, and he caught her hand again.

"See," he said. "Keep your mind on the matter at hand."

"Which matter?"

"Kissing."

"I was not aware that kissing took any great intellect."

"On the contrary," Samuel said again leaning into her. "Anything done well, takes attention."

"It doesn't," she whispered.

"You are wrong, Milady; you are so wrong." His hand tightened on hers and his breath was hot against her lips.

Amelia gave up fighting him. If he thought her straggling hair becoming, she would not disillusion him. He tipped her face to his. He did kiss her then, and she thought of nothing but his lips on hers. Heat fluttered through her. This was madness, she thought. This was folly for she feared Commander Samuel Beresford had taken her fancy to an alarming degree.

When the carriage rolled to a stop, she searched futilely for her discarded bonnet. Samuel found it and placed it on her rumpled curls, tying it gently beneath her chin.

Samuel adjusted the bow, just so, to the side of her face, as carefully as a serving maid would do, and she had the sudden feeling that he had tied another girl's bonnet after kissing her. Anger filled her. She had no right to be angry, she told herself.

They were not truly engaged, but he keeps kissing me, she thought. And you keep letting him, the contrary voice of her conscience said. "I am Lady Amelia Atherton," she told herself. "I am not some common woman he can toy with. I have to find my dignity. I have to pull myself together and stop letting his kisses affect me so. I shall at this very moment. How dare he think he can just kiss me whenever he likes!" She summoned a sense of outrage and held on to it.

Commander Beresford let go of her hand, straightened his jacket and stood. He jumped out of the carriage and held out a hand to help her descend. When she had recovered herself, she took his hand. She wished she could stomp away, but if she fell in the mud in the street she could not be very convincingly angry.

She found that her heart was fluttering and she had trouble concentrating on disembarking. She nearly lost her footing, but his strong arms held her steady as the footman came forward somewhat belatedly to attend the carriage door.

"Concentrate, Lady Amelia, on the task at hand," he quipped, once again glib.

How could he be so intense one moment and back to levity the next? At last Amelia was beginning to understand. In the past weeks she had gained some insight into the mind of Commander Beresford, and she saw that he viewed life as a game but his flippancy was the ruse. He rarely showed his true feelings. She found she recognized the sensation; until recently she had done the same. She had been called cold. It had caused those she cared about to doubt her affections.

His gaze fixed on her, unwavering, as she exited the carriage, as if his face was nothing more than a mask set in place. It was the still visage of the Commander that allowed his men to read nothing of his heart, like the surface of the ocean, hiding the depths, only she now saw the truth.

She smiled sweetly at him as he held her hand. "You want the world to think you are a heartless rake, Commander Beresford, but I think, you are also not unmoved."

He looked at her then, as none of the foppish men in her circle had looked at her. Samuel Beresford truly saw her. She found she could not still her racing heart as she alighted from the carriage.

Samuel took her hand and tucked it possessively around his elbow. They stepped out onto a quiet street. The houses were modestly sized but quite attractive. A four storied house, the stucco a pale shade of pink, caught her eye.

"Well, this one is charming," said Amelia, gazing up at it. There were small balconies fenced in with wrought iron on the second level, and a quaint motif above the door. It was no less respectable than Aunt Ebba's townhouse, just scaled down a bit. "What do you think of it?"

"Garish. How do you like that one?" Samuel gestured

to a house two doors over from the pink stucco. It was a muted shade of grey, with none of the decorative elements that made the other one so lovely.

Amelia shook her head. "Boring. Do you not have an ounce of style, Commander Beresford? You will not want to come home to that. It does not say welcome like this one does. Imagine it, returning from a long naval campaign. Halfway down the street you could see this house, windows aglow, and know that you were home."

She was still gazing up at the house as she spoke, but when she glanced over at Samuel and saw him studying her with an intense look on his face, her cheeks heated. Where had that come from, asking him to imagine their life together? Their engagement was still a pretense. Amelia dropped her gaze to the uneven paving stones. He stepped up behind her and took her hand, waiting until she looked up at him to speak.

"I can imagine it, Lady Amelia Atherton. Can you?" he said, voice husky with emotion.

Amelia's throat was dry, her palms sweating beneath her kid-skin gloves. She looked to Samuel, then back at the house.

"I can," she said, barely more than a whisper.

Samuel grinned. He brought her hand to his lips and kissed her knuckles. "Not at this house, of course. Ugly thing," he said with a dramatic flair as they walked arm in arm to the carriage.

They had to wait a moment while the tardy footman jumped forward to open the door for them.

She shook off the domestic feeling as the carriage pulled away from the townhouse. It's only a ruse, she told herself. She was getting caught up in the fiction of their affair. She had to remember why she was in London. "Why did we not go to the docks?" she asked. "I thought we were only viewing townhouses as an artifice? What about my father?"

"I am already investigating it," he said enigmatically.

"I don't see it," she countered. "You thought there would be some contraband. It is all well and good, to make an excuse for our carriage ride today, but we are not in truth purchasing a townhouse." She wondered why saying those words aloud caused a tremor in her soul. "It's only a pretense," she said, trying to convince herself.

"We cannot go to the docks," he said. "It is not a section of town a lady would frequent. You would have vapors."

"I do not have vapors," she said.

"Then I suppose I merely imagined your fainting; perhaps I simply dreamed of you in my arms." His eyes were twinkling in jest.

So it was Samuel who carried her to her room after she fainted in her Father's study. The thought made her blush. "Pray, do not tease me further," she said.

"I shall not; I certainly can see the cause of your distress, but we would not buy a house there," he argued. "There is no reason for us to go down by the docks."

"Then we shall have to pretend to be lost."

"I do not get lost," he said.

"You are a sailor," Amelia said sweetly. "Would you not like a home close to the port?"

"I would not live there," he said coolly. "Certainly you would not. It's a warehouse district. The houses there are barely more than hovels. We would be mad to look for accommodation there, and as many things as the *Ton* may think of us, no one would think us mad."

She was quiet for a moment. "And yet, people will believe you are stretching your funds beyond their limits to keep your new bride happy," said Amelia. "Is that not mad?"

He looked at her suddenly serious. "Is that the sort of thing you would require? The nicest house on the nicest street and the most expensive furnishings? Grandiose parties every night?" he asked. "Would that be necessary to your happiness?"

Once Amelia would have said yes without hesitation. Those were all of the things she wanted, and had believed she needed. Now, she was not certain. The loss of everything had been a shock, but she hardly thought of her old life now, it seemed as if it belonged to another girl; a silly child. Her country home, now her Uncle Declan's, had seemed alien, while Samuel's family's country home was warm and comfortable. Still, she wanted to clear her father's name, and if he was truly murdered as she thought, she wanted that murderer caught and punished. But nothing could bring him back to her, she thought. She could only go forward, only which way was that?

"No, but that is what people will believe of me," she said at last, and hoped he would leave it at that. She wanted justice for her father, and for herself, she wanted love. Real love; she had lost that when her father died and she saw now that it was all she truly desired.

Had she meant what she had said, about not needing

the most extravagant life? Samuel wondered. His father would certainly not begrudge him one of the smaller estates in the country, and he could afford a modest townhouse, but it would not be what she had grown up with. If she could truly be happy with just... what was he thinking? He could not even think of a wife, any wife, until he at least made captain, and even if she was content with less, she would not wish to be the wife of a naval officer. Lady Amelia was not the type of woman to be alone for months at a time. No woman would want that. He had come to grips with that long ago. Still, he could not help imagining returning home from the sea and seeing her at the front door, perhaps with a child in her arms.

"What is this place?" she asked as the carriage stopped again.

"You will like this one," Samuel had said to Amelia.

He had, against his better judgement instructed the driver to go to the address Percival had given him; the address of the townhouse that already belonged to his brother. It was a classic white brick with a balcony and wonderful lattice work. Flowers in boxes seemed to bloom just for them. For just a moment, Amelia stood spell bound, a small 'o' on her lips. It was still small, but quite elegant. He had wanted to impress her, and he supposed he had.

"Oh," she said again, and started up the stairs to the door. The interior was as beautiful as the exterior, and once Samuel saw the intricate woodwork inside he began to suspect that he would not be able to afford this townhouse at all on his commander's stipend. Percival must have spent a fortune on it. As Amelia walked through it exclaiming about the beauty of this room or that, he wondered how he was going to tell Amelia. Then he thought, it was all a ruse anyway. She would never marry a simple commander. What did it matter?

21

Samuel and Amelia had just returned to Aunt Ebba's and had not even had time to refresh themselves when a servant brought a letter on a silver tray to Amelia. She frowned. She wasn't expecting any correspondence.

"It is from your uncle, the duke," the servant said, having recognized the seal. "It came earlier this afternoon."

Amelia looked at it herself, feeling a slight shiver as she broke the wax seal. This morning with Samuel, she had almost managed to forget about her Uncle Declan. Her knuckles went completely white as she read and she sank down into one of the straight backed parlor chairs.

"What is it?" Samuel asked.

"He has invited me for tea," she said. "Summons, really, and he says since you will be speaking to him about our engagement on the morrow, I should take up residence at his townhouse."

"Well, we shall just tell him you prefer to stay with Aunt Ebba." Samuel held out his hand, and she passed the letter to him, and he read for himself. "I will accompany you," he said.

"He didn't extend an invitation to you," Amelia said.

"I don't suppose you could send him your regrets," said Samuel.

Amelia shook her head. "I don't want to antagonize him."

Samuel caught her hand. "It will be alright. I was going to see him upon the morrow. It appears we shall merely have our discourse a bit early. That is all." Samuel turned to the footman. "Have my man ride to my father's house, and tell the Lord Blackburn and Lord Beresford that our plans have changed. Lady Amelia and I will be having tea with the Duke of Ely today rather than on the morrow."

Amelia had freshened herself, but no amount of powder or cool water could stop her unease. She hoped that Samuel only thought of it as a sort of glow, but she herself felt as if her dress were limp with nervous perspiration. She held no illusion that her uncle was summoning her simply because he missed her company. No. What was particularly vexatious was that he wanted her at his townhouse, and under his thumb. She was nearly terrified.

"He killed my father," Amelia told Samuel. "I know he did."

"I am afraid you may be right," Samuel said. "I had hoped to spare you this meeting."

"I know," she said.

"How well does your uncle know you," Samuel asked after they resettled themselves in the carriage.

"Not well," Amelia admitted wrapping one gloved hand over the other and wringing them together. "I've only spoken to him once since father's death. Before that, we barely saw one another. As a child, I saw him perhaps only half dozen times. He and my father were not close."

"Good," Samuel said squeezing her hand and stilling it. "Then he doesn't know how resourceful you are. You are the diamond of the *Ton*," he reminded her. "You are strong and smart and beautiful. You can do this."

"I thought men didn't like smart women," she blurted just as the carriage lurched to a halt. She gave a little squeak of fear.

"Just be calm. I will not leave you there." He gripped her hand tightly. "I swear it." His eyes were very serious, and she wished she could just hide her head against his strong shoulder. Amelia could not think how he would be able to help her if her uncle demanded her obedience.

"Just remember that the new Duke also doesn't know that Percy is well, or in London. That is also to our advantage."

Amelia nodded and lifted her chin as if she were about to do battle. She supposed she was.

The parlor was just as she remembered it, furnished with somber elegance. The high-backed chairs where her father had sat and read her fairy stories before the fire, were unmoved, and the gilded ceiling that had impressed both friends and suitors alike still bespoke of home, and yet, it was no longer home.

Her Uncle Declan was as she remembered him too,

impeccably and conservatively dressed. The grey in his hair gave him a dignified look that was so much a sham. He should have looked worn and weary, as her father did on his last days. Amelia felt a tremor of anger pass through her. Only Samuel's hand at her elbow kept her grounded.

Her uncle looked at her as if he held her in contempt, and it was all she could do to remember her manners. She dropped into a short curtsey, her black crepe rustling as it brushed the floor. "Your Grace." She murmured. The epilation that belonged to her deceased father was bitter on her tongue.

"I thought we would take tea in the morning room," the duke said. Her uncle directed them to sit and called for refreshment as if this were a social call.

"Your invitation was unexpected," Samuel said, as if he had actually been invited.

The duke did not correct him, only a slight frown forming on his brow.

Amelia felt a hard knot beginning to form in her stomach as they spoke. Her eyes traveled across the room to the hateful figure of her uncle and endeavored to cover her loathing with a small smile.

Pleasantries were exchanged, Samuel speaking condolences for the death of the duke's brother and the duke did the same for Percival's illness, but his glowering façade never changed.

"Is Lord Beresford expected to recover?" The duke asked of Samuel, and Amelia looked up interested. The duke had taken the bait then. Now, all they had to do was catch the fish. She knew Samuel had some plan, but she did not have the details of it, and her heart was racing with fear.

Samuel shook his head. "Poor Percival," he said in a cool voice and then deftly changed the subject as if Lord Beresford mattered not a whit. "But I had hoped to speak of happier tidings," Samuel said. "I expected to come on the morrow to ask your permission to wed your niece," Samuel continued as he lounged easily in the chair beside Amelia.

Amelia perched nervously on the edge as her uncle's man brought the tea service. A second servant brought cakes. Amelia knew neither of them.

"Permission?" said the duke sourly. "It would seem you have eschewed my wishes entirely. I thought you had already announced."

"Nothing of the sort," Samuel said as he stirred his tea. "You know how women are. One letter to a friend and the whole of London knows."

"Is that the truth of it?" the duke asked glaring at Amelia.

"I beg your pardon," Amelia said. "I was only so overwhelmed with joy." She forced the teacup to her lips, thoughts of poison dancing in her head.

"So a love match?" the duke inquired of Samuel. Her uncle looked incredulous.

Amelia sucked in her breath wondering how Samuel would answer. He shrugged off the question.

"Would that surprise you, Your Grace?" Samuel asked.

"Truly yes. When half of London's whelps were howling at her skirts just a few months ago, and yet you were absent then. But now...now after the Livingston's Ball you come snooping around my niece and ward."

"She was not yet your ward at the ball," Samuel said.

"No, she was not," her uncle replied silkily.

"Now, you are asking my permission not to court her, but to marry her?" her uncle repeated. "Does it not seem hasty? Now, when all of London already knows of your intentions—all excepting me. You think to force my hand? To foist yourself upon my family?"

Amelia thought that considering how poorly the duke treated his family, she couldn't imagine anyone voluntarily wishing to be a part of it, but Samuel didn't reference her father's death directly. She shifted furtively out of the duke's direct line of sight. She hoped that he had forgotten her.

"Oh, you mistake me," Samuel said evenly. "I would have sent word to you sooner had I known the extent of my lady's friendships and their nattering. Indeed, I am very pleased to officially ask for the hand of your niece..." he paused meaningfully. "And of course to thank you, Your Grace."

"Thank me? For what, pray?"

"Why for my eminent earldom of course," Samuel said, picking up the teacup and studying it as if reading the leaves. He paused meaningfully and then looked at the duke. "You know, younger brother to younger brother, I would have been happy with a captaincy, but I suppose my brother was troublesome. He was habitually so. If I can keep your confidence, I thought about poisoning him myself many time, and now the deed is done." Samuel tipped his cup to the duke as if toasting with champagne.

"Whatever do you mean?" the duke said glancing surreptitiously at Amelia and committing to nothing.

Amelia buried her eyes in her teacup, playing the demure miss. She could not chance her uncle seeing the loathing in her face.

"I mean my brother was poisoned, of course," Samuel said.

"I heard something to that effect. Ghastly. An accident?"

"No."

"How awful. Do you know who did it?"

"Yes, as a matter of fact. I have known for some time now. I even know why."

"But I have heard nothing of your brother's death," the duke said.

"He lingers," Samuel admitted. "Poor chap."

Amelia sat demolishing a sweet cake with her fork, not at all sure she should add to this conversation or if the duke even remembered she was there. Samuel had sprung his trap all that was left now was to see if the duke would be caught. His dark eyes were on Samuel, weighing him. Samuel took another sip of tea. It had to have gone cold. Hers was. She always thought Samuel was impatient a man and in need of restraint. Now she saw he was not. She was surprised, he seemed to be weighing the duke and biding his time. The room was fraught with tension, and she dared not move, lest she break it.

"What do you want?" The duke said at last.

"I would ask to be treated like family, but well, that

may not be the most apropos turn of phrase," Samuel answered dismissively.

Amelia gasped. It would not do to take such chances with the duke, and she feared for Samuel and his flippantness.

The duke did not look at her. "Amelia," he said softly, "Your room is ready for you. You should retire."

Amelia froze momentarily with the unexpected address. Terror rushed through her in a heartbeat. She could not be dismissed. She could not leave Samuel. "But Uncle," she said with forced brightness. "I have not finished my cake." She shoved a bite of the broken morsels into her mouth and tried to chew the dry crumbs. It was an inane excuse and she really didn't expect it to work. Even her uncle could not think she was such a lack-a-wit.

Her uncle ignored her, rang for the servant, and said, "Lady Amelia is tired. Please escort her to her room."

The dour woman curtseyed. "Yes, Your Grace," she said, taking Amelia by the arm.

Amelia stood, but shot a desperate look at Samuel. He had said he would not leave her here. He had promised.

"Let your niece go back to her Aunt Ebba's," Samuel said, standing and moving to her. "The sweet lady is expecting her. She will worry."

"It is a simple matter to send a note to her aunt," her uncle said. "Amelia stays."

Amelia bristled. She simply could not play the ninny any longer. "You won't get away with this," she snapped pulling away from the woman and moving closer to Samuel.

Samuel gripped her shoulder hard and she nearly cried out. Instead, she bit her lip, going silent.

"Pray? Get away with what?" The duke asked. When she didn't answer, her uncle said, "Young ladies are not to poke their noses into men's business, but you did, didn't you? You found the book. You were never intended to find that, my dear. It is not your concern. You will give it back to me."

"I don't know what you mean," Amelia stammered. So he had known of the cypher book and searched for it; not just the study, but throughout the house and came to the conclusion that if it were not there Amelia must have it in her possession.

"Do not try my patience," The duke said coldly as Samuel stepped forward and attempted to corral Amelia safely behind him. "You have meddled where you don't belong, I am afraid," the duke continued.

"You are a horrible, odious man," Amelia snapped.

"Careful little one," her uncle said, catching her arm. "Your fate is tied with mine now. I am the Duke of Ely."

"I have the book," Samuel interrupted. "She knows nothing. She is only a woman, and as expected, she brought the book to a man for advice. Let her be."

"If you want Amelia," her uncle said succinctly, "I want the book."

"Done," Samuel agreed. "Amelia, go to the carriage."

Her uncle did not release her. "No, no," her uncle said. "She stays right here."

"You can't keep me," Amelia said.

"Oh on the contrary, little one, I can do whatever I like with you. You are my niece and my responsibility since the demise of my dear brother. If I want to lock you up in your room or lock you up in Bedlam, it is my right."

Amelia blanched and then anger boiled up in her. She leveled a sharp kick to his shins, and dragged her arm away from him, attempting to pull free.

Her uncle's face purpled. He raised a hand as if to strike her and Samuel intervened grabbing his arm causing him to release Amelia. "Not while I have breath in my body, sir," Samuel spat. "We may do business, but you will not strike her. I don't care if you are a duke."

In an instant another serving man was in the room, and Amelia realized the man was not a footman at all. He out sized Samuel and pulled him unceremoniously off of the duke. She screamed, "What are you doing?"

The duke straightened his cravat and pulled the cuffs of his sleeves down so they peeked from beneath his impeccable jacket. "Now, if you can both be civil," he said. "Let him go, Roberts. He is my guest. My nieces' betrothed. The son of the Earl of Blackburn," the duke said.

The man, Roberts, released Samuel and went to stand by the door as the duke looked at Amelia with consternation.

"Jean," the duke said addressing the maid who had stood back against the wall. "Take Lady Amelia to her room, now."

Amelia raised her head a little. "Very well," she said. "But I am not staying here, Uncle. I am going back to Aunt Ebba's."

He didn't answer her.

She walked down the corridor, with the dour serving

woman, her mind racing ahead to the front door. Surely she could get past one maid. As they passed the music room, she shoved the woman into the room and wrenched the door shut with all her might. She picked up her skirts and ran; bolting for the door and the carriage. Amelia nearly made it down the front steps before her uncle's large footman caught up with her and swept her off of her feet.

What happened next occurred with such speed that she was uncertain when her body had changed hands. One moment her uncle's man had her, and the next she was wrested from his grasp and into the arms of the footman who had helped her into Samuel's carriage earlier that day. Carlton was his name she remembered belatedly. His unusually strong arm was muscled under her. She realized that Carlton was definitely not Samuel's regular footman. He was rougher somehow. Now he carried her to the carriage, with hands that held the surety of one who handled the ropes of a sail. She realized that Samuel had planned for trouble.

"We'll get you to safety M'lady," Carlton said.

Once again she was helped into the conveyance, but with nothing so gentle as a hand up. Instead she was summarily tossed into the carriage, breathless, but out of danger. No sooner was Amelia inside than the carriage gave a great lurch as if something had struck it and she tumbled to the floor in a flurry of skirts.

Her thoughts were screaming. She could not leave Samuel behind with the man who killed her father! What started as a wonderful day had ended in disaster. She did not know what to do. All she could think was get help. She glanced desperately at Samuel's footman, hoping to send someone for aid, when she realized that there was a second man, even burlier than the fellow who had helped her exit the carriage all day: he was actually quite appalling as a footman, but both were quite grand as bodyguards. The second of Samuel's men hoisted the unconscious Roberts up on his shoulder as if he were light as a deer and strode towards the carriage.

"Sorry M'lady," he said as the two men proceeded to drag the duke's man inside. Carlton boarded the carriage as Amelia struggled to her feet. "We have nowhere else to put him until the Watch gets here and I'm afraid he'd attract attention on the street."

"Samuel!" she said. The carriage lurched forward again. She had still not gotten her footing. Roberts was sprawled unconscious on one seat and Carlton, was smiling at her from the other.

"No. No. No," she said frantic. "We can't leave Samuel with my uncle. He killed my father. He cannot take Samuel from me too!"

"Do not worry, yourself" Carlton said. "The Commander's brother, Lord Beresford has just returned from securing the docks. He and the boys will be here quick as I drawed this one's cork." He gestured to the fallen Roberts. "The duke isn't going anywhere but the gaol."

There was a great shuffling outside and Amelia, too curious for her own good, peered out of the carriage. She recognized Percival with some members of the watch. "Lord Beresford," she called with an indecorous shout.

Percival was talking animatedly with one of the

footman and an older gentleman who she did not immediately recognize. Then the older gentleman turned, headed straight for the carriage, and poked his head inside.

"Lady Amelia," he said. "Your pardon for speaking so frankly, when we have not been introduced, but I need to know, how many men are holding my son?"

"I don't know," she stammered. "I only saw the duke and the one other." She gestured and he saw her uncle's man still spread unconscious on the opposite seat. The gentleman muttered under his breath, and said. "Let us find you another carriage. Lady Patience is at my townhouse with my wife, I believe," he said as he took her arm to escort her.

She slapped his hand away. "I'm not going anywhere," she snapped, eyes flashing fire. "Samuel is in danger and I'm not leaving him."

22

*I*nside the townhouse, Samuel watched the duke for a long moment. The maid left the room with Amelia, and although he didn't like it, he knew that as long as the duke was with him, she wouldn't be in immediate danger. He had wished she had gotten to the carriage and his men, but he trusted her to be resourceful if necessary.

The duke had poured himself a brandy. He did not offer any to Samuel. He took a long swallow and set the glass aside. "You should not have threatened me," he said.

"You should not have threatened my intended," Samuel retorted.

A loud clatter was heard in the corridor and a door slammed with enough force to rattle the windows loose. Samuel gave the duke a small shrug. "It seems Amelia did not wish to retire," he said.

"Get her," the duke said, and the large man followed, leaving the duke alone with Samuel.

Samuel stood in one fluid motion and sat his teacup carefully on the table. He moved towards the door that the footman had gone out of, following Amelia, but the duke stood in his way. For all that he was a villain, he was a member of the Peerage, Samuel reminded himself, allowing a moment of pause. He listened with half an ear to the scuffle outside and he was fairly certain his men had Amelia safe.

"Sit down," the duke barked at him. "You do not understand. You are nothing but a common seaman. You cannot touch me. This ends now."

"Oh, I agree," Samuel said, a gleam, of amusement in his eye. "But I am afraid it is you who is uninformed, Your Grace. You see. I really cannot figure how you will explain another body," Samuel objected. "Or the gold, or the fact that I have the book. No, killing me would be a grave mistake."

"The book is in your possession," the duke said. "I don't need to kill you. Just discredit you. It solves both of my problems.

"And Amelia?"

"Bedlam. It is understandable she would be so distraught; with the death of both her father and her new fiancé. No one will question it."

"Even dukes are not invulnerable, as you well know," Samuel said.

"You forget yourself," the duke said softly.

"Do I?" Samuel said. "Or do you forget I am quite good at capturing traitors to the crown."

"You have no recourse, Commander. Here is the brash Samuel Beresford, the unloved son, the son so intent upon nothing but his naval career, strangely showing his face at a ball for his betters…"

Samuel's jaw tightened momentarily, and then softened.

"I was accompanying my brother," Samuel began.

"Exactly," the duke said. "Everyone at the ball saw you with Lord Beresford."

"Of course I was with my brother," Samuel said.

"All present saw you with your brother, and all saw you practically bowl over poor Lord Cornishe to dance with my niece…to ingratiate yourself with the late duke's daughter. My own dear brother, was pulled into this plot by you, and then, you absent yourself from the event at just the time when Lord Beresford became ill."

"I took my brother home," Samuel protested.

"You conveniently spirited him away to the country, just when he was poisoned. I think it is quite clear that you are the one who did the deed."

"What?" Samuel said. "You are mad. No one will believe it."

"Wouldn't they? Do you think they would believe the word of a second son over a duke? I think not. If they didn't believe your brother, they certainly won't believe you."

"I think they will believe me now," Percival said standing in the doorway, a gun leveled on the duke. "Now, unhand my brother, you blackguard."

"But you were dead – at death's door," the duke stuttered as Percy and several men of watch advanced on him. "The rumors –"

"My demise was greatly over exaggerated," Percival

said continuing to hold the gun on the duke as the men of the Watch entered the room.

"Nothing so simple as a letter from a woman to her friend. It takes so little to start gossip," Samuel said, tutting. He turned to his brother. "Is all in order?" he asked. "Do we have evidence to prove him a traitor to the crown?"

"Enough for him to hang five times over," Percival said. "Boxes of gold bars with the royal seal, the ship's manifest and past shipments in his own hand as well as money to his private accounts."

"A moment then," Samuel said to the watch who were in the process of binding the duke's hands as he shouted his innocence.

"Your Grace," he said politely. "This is for the heartache you caused Lady Amelia." Samuel hauled back and punched the duke, knocking him completely senseless, and mercifully quiet. Samuel rubbed his knuckles. "I've been wanting to do that for ages," He explained to his brother. "I couldn't strike a duke, but a traitor; I could hit a traitor."

Percy laughed and threw an arm over his brother's shoulder. "Come, your lady awaits."

"You were supposed to see her home," Samuel protested.

"Seeing Lady Amelia anywhere that she does not intend to go is quite the feat," Percy said. "I do believe you have found a woman who is even more irascible than mother."

LADY AMELIA ATHERTON was pacing on the street. Her slippers were ruined; her hem was soiled but no one could convince her to be conveyed home without Commander Beresford. In fact, she refused to sit in a carriage at all, and the only thing that kept her from running to Samuel's rescue was the fact that she knew she would only cause him more distress if she reentered the townhouse.

Just then, she saw someone exit the townhouse. She recognized him instantly as Samuel, and cried out. When he reached her, he enfolded her in his arms most indecorously. For a moment she was caught up in the scent of him, the warmth of his body and the strength of his arms. Amelia shivered. "He could have killed you too," she said.

"Did you have so little faith in me?"

She didn't answer and it felt like a betrayal.

"Hmmm? Well," he said surprised. "Something has finally rendered the indomitable Lady Amelia speechless."

"I was afraid," she whispered in a barely audible voice. "I was afraid I would lose you too."

He tipped her bonnet and kissed her on her forehead, his lips lingering.

She was so relieved that he was alright, she could think of nothing but his nearness, and then she realized that others had gathered around them.

Her hand went to her hair, straggling from beneath her hat. She was in a horrid state.

Samuel cleared his throat and she stepped quickly away, but Samuel kept her hand on his arm steadying her as he turned to the others.

"We have him," Samuel said to his father. "He practically admitted to poisoning Percy and the murder of his brother, The late Duke of Ely to protect his secrets."

"Well, it answers our question as to what sort of contraband would incite murder," Percival added. "If you are already going to hang for treason; you may as well hang for murder."

Samuel nodded, holding Amelia close. She had begun to shake.

"Samuel," said the older man, surprised. "I underestimated you, and your lady. You did well."

"Thank you, Father."

Father! Amelia choked. She looked from one to the other, realizing at long last that the older man who had asked about Samuel earlier was Samuel's father, the Earl of Blackburn. She had spoken so sharply to him. Her hand went to her mouth as she realized how horrible she had been. How could she have missed the resemblance? Both were large boned and strong. Both had that peculiar calm and now she realized the gentleman had called Samuel his son when he spoke to her, but she had not even heard him. Amelia's hand went to her bonnet attempting to stow several more stray hairs underneath it and put some order to her appearance, but it was much too late to worry about that.

"Lord Blackburn," she said, blushing hotly.

"You should take your fiancée home," the earl

continued. "There's been enough excitement here. She looks like to swoon."

"Yes, father, I shall take her back to her aunt's forthwith, but for your future reference, my fiancé, is not prone to swooning."

"And if you do," he whispered for her ears only. "I shall catch you."

A secret smile passed her lips.

"Her Aunt Ebba is with Lady Patience at father's townhouse," said Percival, gesturing towards his carriage. "And so is Mother. You were right, Samuel. She did not stay in Bath, but has descended upon us like a raging lioness."

Samuel grinned an *I told you so,* look that Amelia had begun to recognize as something that often passed between the brothers. Within the teasing, was love, something she never remembered seeing between her own father and her uncle, something she hoped for her own children. Where had that thought come from? She glanced at Samuel, but he was unaware of the direction of her thoughts.

"Take my carriage," Percival said to Samuel. "Father and I will finish here."

"I will inform Mother of your health," Samuel promised.

"Tell her we will be home in time for tea," Percy said. "Or perhaps dinner..."

"I believe I've had quite enough tea," Amelia said thinking of the awful meeting with her uncle.

"I believe I will have something a little stronger than tea," Samuel added at the same time as Amelia spoke.

They smiled at each other and Samuel helped Amelia into the carriage. She was glad for a moment of privacy.

Samuel and Amelia took Percy's carriage while Samuel's brother rode with his father, since Samuel's carriage was occupied with the still unconscious Roberts.

Samuel leaned against the back of the carriage and rubbed his knuckles with a satisfied sigh. "I have to admit," he said. "It felt quite good to hit the man who caused you so much pain." He grinned at Amelia for a moment and then slipped his arm around Amelia's shoulders, pulling her close against him. She stiffened, as if to pull away, but then, with a quiet *tut* settled into the crook of his shoulder. She really should not, but she was so shaken by the encounter with her uncle and what it all meant, not just for her but for all of London, that she could not resist.

All of the implications of the duke being her guardian came crashing down on her. She would be with her Aunt Ebba now, but she thought that Amelia was to marry Commander Beresford, what would happen when their ruse came to light? She prided herself on her aplomb, but she could not stop shaking.

"What if he somehow escapes?" she said. "He's a duke. He has influence." She could be at the mercy of the man who killed her father.

"No," Samuel said, riding the exhilaration of his recent victory. "That will not happen. He is a traitor. He's attacked two members of the Peerage, and killed one; all to cover his theft from the crown. We have witnesses to his villainy and a warehouse full of gold. He will not escape his comeuppance. This, my dear is the difference between a naval officer and pirate," he said with a smile.

She shuddered. "I shall never call you a pirate again, even in jest" she said. "But, what will it all mean? He was still my guardian...and now..."

"Now, I don't need his approval of our union," said Samuel his silly grin, breaking into an all-out laugh.

She stared at him as he laughed.

"Our false union," Amelia whispered. "Commander Beresford. Oh, Commander Beresford, stop," she admonished trying to bring him back to earth.

Samuel sobered at her words and the formal address. He could see her rebuff now in her serious face, and all the elation of his win left him. It was exactly as he told his brother so long ago. She didn't love him. She didn't want to marry him. She only wanted to clear her father's name, and now she had done that. It was finished.

Pain ripped through him at the thought. She could go back to being the toast of Town. She could go back to her parties and dangling favors before all the Peerage. Only he wasn't one of her dandies to be toyed with and never was. He was only a commander and she was the diamond of the *Ton*.

As he looked at her serious face, he realized, he no longer believed that she was the vapid woman he once thought her. Perhaps she never was.

And now, he had caught a traitor. He may be a second son, but he was still a man to be reckoned with. The betrothal may have started out as a ruse, but he had become accustomed to the Lady Amelia Atherton at his side. He liked her there. He wasn't about to give her up.

Hadn't he once said that if he ever decided to marry, no one would ever stop him?

"Why, Lady Amelia, I thought we were on a first name basis," he said flippantly. "After all, I am going to marry you."

Amelia huffed, and then realized what he had said. He said he was going to marry her.

"Really," she said sardonically. "You are going to marry me?" She raised her chin a little. "You haven't asked me."

"I did," he said, turning her face to him. "Well, actually…"

"I didn't say yes."

"Of course you did," he replied, "You asked me…and I said yes." He said very seriously and kissed her open astonished mouth. For a moment she melted and then she placed her hands on his chest and pushed.

"Stop," she said. "If someone sees us…"

"What? You will be ruined? You would have to marry me?"

She looked at him for a moment startled by this truth. "Well. Very well then, Commander, carry on," she said tipping her face up to him.

23

The carriage stopped and Amelia tried to smooth her rumpled dress. It had been quite an eventful day. Her heart was still pounding from the thought of being at the mercy of her father's murderer, and the whirl wind of house viewings, and, Samuel's kisses in the carriage, and the final truth, that she didn't want their sham of a betrothal any more. She wanted the real thing. She wanted Commander Samuel Beresford, even if he never made captain, she wanted him, and he wanted her.

It was quite a relief to realize that he was smart enough to figure things out for himself without her leading him. He had proven that she could depend upon him and he cut quite a figure even if he was less fine than was fashionable. She considered him handsome in a virile sort of way, and her opinion was the only one that counted. A thrill went through her. He was going to be her husband, she thought. Hers. She would have liked to announce their new engagement, now solidified in the carriage; to sing it from the rooftops, but of course, that time had already passed. The celebration of her engagement would have to be shared with the celebration of her uncle's capture.

When Samuel opened the door of the carriage, and Amelia looked out on the lawn, she was surprised by the number of carriages. "Is your family entertaining?" she asked. "I cannot be seen like this, Samuel." She contemplated having him sneak her in a servant's entrance so she could make herself somewhat presentable.

"No," Samuel said. "Most of this is my mother's retinue. My mother's and my father's," Samuel said with a frown. "They do not often reside in the same house."

Amelia would have liked to meet her future mother-in-law under better circumstances than she had met her father-in-law, but there was no help for it.

"She must pack like Aunt Ebba," Amelia said to break the tension. Samuel smiled at her. "Do not fret," he said encouragingly. "She will love you."

Samuel did allow her a moment to wash her face and repin her hair. She noticed that her eyes were bright and the dark circles had gone. She was not so bedraggled as she had thought. In fact, she was almost her former beauty, although her gown was a bit travel worn and her slippers were completely ruined. Amelia fortified herself to meet Samuel's parents but it was not as taxing as she thought it would be. Patience and Aunt Ebba were there, discussing fashion and wedding plans with Lady Blackburn.

The wife of the Earl of Blackburn, and Samuel's mother, was a compact vivacious woman who flitted from Patience to Amelia like a small bird, with copies of Ackermann's latest fashion plates in hand. They already had tea on the table but Lady Blackburn called for a new pot to accommodate Amelia and Samuel. Samuel paused holding a brandy decanter. Instead of pouring, he closed it and returned to the table for tea. He and Amelia exchanged a glance. To Amelia, nothing tasted quite so good as hot tea with cream and sugar even with today's excursion nothing could spoil the beverage.

She sipped blissfully as Lady Blackburn spoke, "Lady Patience will marry my Percival first of course," she said.

"Oh Patience, how wonderful," Amelia said. "When did Lord Beresford propose?"

"He hasn't actually spoken the words yet," she said embarrassed. "But he did speak to his father, and so Lady Blackburn says I needn't worry."

Lady Patience surely would not do as Amelia had done and take matters into her own hands, Amelia thought. She wondered if she should speak to Samuel about his brother's tardiness and threw him a glance.

"Well, Mother," Samuel added. "Percy could not very well ride into London to ask for the lady's hand in marriage when the Duke of Ely and most of London thought that he was on his way to an early grave until just recently."

Patience went a little white at the very thought and Aunt Ebba patted her hand.

In no time at all Percival arrived with Samuel's father and the Earl and Lady Blackburn called for dinner to be served. Amelia now realized that the earl looked almost exactly like Samuel with a stouter build and graying hair. He spoke briefly to Amelia to welcome her to the family and thank her for her steadfastness this afternoon. He also remarked that he was glad that someone had been able to get his son Samuel off of that boat. Amelia wasn't quite sure that was so, but before she could answer, Samuel interrupted.

"It's a ship," Samuel corrected, "And my ship mates were bloody helpful this afternoon, Father."

His father leveled a gaze at Samuel and admonished him for his language in front of the ladies.

"I think Samuel was brilliant," Percival interrupted. "I'm sure Samuel will receive his captaincy now; perhaps even a knighthood, don't you agree, Father?

"I do," the earl said foregoing tea and pouring himself a glass of brandy.

"You do?" Samuel asked. "You agree, Father? Is the world coming to an end?"

"It might be," he said exchanging a look with Lady Blackburn. "Your mother and I are in the same house."

Although it was considered gauche to partner with one's spouse at dinner, the Earl of Blackburn gave her his arm and escorted his wife into dinner, followed by Amelia and Samuel and the others.

"Whatever was the duke thinking," the earl asked as the footman served a superb chestnut soup. "Surely he had to know he couldn't get away with murder."

"From what I was able to glean, both from records and from my brief discussion with your father," Percy said with a nod to Amelia. "Your Uncle Declan always lived somewhat beyond his means. When, the former duke refused to continue to support his lifestyle, he ran up a debt, some of it in your father's name. When the late duke refused to pay his brother's debts, their association became strained. Apparently Lady Amelia was very young at this point," Percival said.

"So this has been going on for years," Amelia said. "No wonder there was such animosity between them."

"No doubt," Percy agreed. "Then, he fell in with a group of conspirators who supported Napoleon rather than the true king. Can you imagine?"

"Lud," Aunt Ebba said, a hand to her mouth.

"When funds from the Crown were sent to France, they siphoned off a number of gold bars thinking that the Crown, would not know of its loss, but your father found out about the theft, and confronted Declan."

"Let's do talk of something more pleasant," Patience urged, placing a hand on Percy's wrist.

"And well, you know the rest" Percival concluded with a nod to Amelia.

Conversation returned to fashion and weddings.

TEN MONTHS LATER

AMELIA SAT at the piano playing the last interlude of her piece. It seemed an appropriate piece to play on her wedding day.

"We should be going, Amelia," said Patience. She had a new confidence since Percival had proposed, and it pleased Amelia to see her friend standing so tall, and meeting people's eyes without flinching.

"You are right, I know. It would not do to be late to my own wedding, though I would like to keep Commander Beresford waiting, wondering if I will attend," said Amelia. She strode from the room behind Patience, and refused to turn back to look a final time. This was the end of this chapter in her life, but there would be plenty of joy in the next one.

"You are so cruel to him. It is a wonder he wants to marry you at all," said Patience. Then she looked Amelia up and down and laughed. "Then again, maybe it is not such a wonder. How splendid that he made Captain so recently, what fine timing."

Fine timing, or Samuel's own grit, Amelia thought.

"Are you nervous?" asked Patience, as they rode side by side in the carriage. The ceremony was to take place in town, at a small parish, with less of the fanfare Amelia had once imagined her wedding would hold. "I would be. Oh, I am nervous for you!"

"I am not nervous," Amelia said. Her insides were twisting like a barrel of snakes and her mind was racing, but it was not nerves. It was excitement, she realized.

SAMUEL WAS NERVOUS. He was sweating an unseemly amount into his spring jacket, and even Percival mocked him.

"Are you going to fidget your way through the entire ceremony," said Percival. "Someone will think you have contracted hives, and your new bride will refuse to touch you."

"Do you remember your wedding day?" Samuel asked.

"Actually, not much," Percival admitted. "I hope that you will be happy, my brother. If you are but half as blissful as I am, you will be blest."

"I like my chances, then" said Samuel.

"All of this because of a bet, and a dance," said Percival, under his breath. "All because she has the same name as your beloved ship. What a thing to start a marriage on."

All conversation ceased when Lady Amelia Atherton stepped into view on her Uncle Edward's arm. Aunt Ebba sniffled in the front row, and dabbed at her eyes as her husband walked Amelia down the aisle. Her young son Phillip sat beside her looking like a miniature version of his father.

Even if he had wanted to speak, Samuel's tongue would have tied itself into knots with the effort. If Amelia had been beautiful before, today she was a goddess. It was not the cut of her dress or the ruffles, though she might think so, nor the curl or sheen of her hair. It was the vulnerability in her face that did it; the nervousness in her smile, and the proud tilt of her chin. He vowed before God that he would do his best to never harm her. Her expression showed she cared about him, about this marriage, and that she had something to lose now. He wanted to tell her she had nothing to worry about, that she could never lose or him. They would weather every storm.

Samuel came to understand what Percival had meant when he said he didn't remember his own wedding. If there were passages read and vows said, Samuel could not remember them. All he could remember was looking down at Amelia and feeling his heart expanding in a painful shock to make room for her there. No, not make room. She was his heart now, and everything else was at her mercy, taking up whatever room she would allow.

"Are you crying?" Amelia asked him, at the end of it all.

"Certainly not," Samuel said, rubbing his eyes. "A bit of dust, that is all. Move along now, or people will think you are gawking over your new husband. Unseemly, isn't it, I thought I married a lady."

"Have a care, or you will soon discover just how thin my ladylike manners are when I am in a passion," said Amelia.

He squeezed her arm, just a bit and when she looked at him, he was wearing that roguish smile that had so enticed her. Her heart did a little flip and would not stop fluttering in her chest.

"My dear wife," he said his voice a soft rumble, just for her ears. "I await your pleasure."

EPILOGUE

*D*ue to the treason of Amelia's Uncle Declan, the title was stripped from the Atherton name and all lands were lost to the crown. Once Amelia would have felt the loss of her childhood home, but now, Samuel himself was all the home she needed; though her title of Lady was restored when Amelia married Samuel Beresford. He had been knighted for services to the Crown in catching the Duke of Ely in his treachery, in addition to obtaining his captaincy.

In town, Lady Charity enjoyed the gossip about Amelia immensely until Patience noted to Charity that if she had managed to snag Amelia's father, as his wife, she also would have lost her title, so in the long run it was best that she never married him. "Upon my word, aren't you the lucky one," Patience said, as she fluttered her fan, just a bit.

When asked if she missed the grand parties of the *Ton*, Amelia said she didn't mind at all. She had her music for the long nights when Samuel was at sea, and mostly had her Captain.

Six months passed and Amelia was once again in the music room playing. She lost herself in the music. Marriage was nothing like what Amelia had expected. Each day was something new, a chance to learn about Samuel and for him to learn about her. Some of those moments were not pleasant, but they were heavily outnumbered by the moments that were. She had made the little house theirs, and on a modest budget. Well, she would call it modest, though Samuel may not and she had settled into life as a wife.

"Amelia, will you come here please?" Samuel asked, for the third time.

Amelia played a little louder. Shortly after they moved in, the cabinet piano her father had given her at the age of twelve had arrived with a brief note from her Aunt Ebba and Uncle Edward. Uncle Edward wrote that he thought the instrument was an appropriate wedding gift for the joy she had given his wife with her company, and he hoped that she would come to stay with Ebba on occasion. With that in mind they had also bought the first piano, the one which she had learned to play on, for their house. However, she should still consider it hers. Amelia had written her Uncle Edward an exuberant thank you letter, saying he restored her faith in family for she loved the piano, and it felt like the last thing she had of her father.

"Amelia," Samuel repeated, and this time it was not a question.

"I don't want you to leave," said Amelia, biting her lip

to keep from crying. Even though she knew that it would be like this, there had been nothing she could do to prepare herself.

"I will have to leave either way; it is just whether or not we have a chance at farewell before I do," said Samuel, voice soothing. He stepped into the music room in his smart uniform with its gold buttons and epaulets of rank, looking regal and authoritative and downright dashing.

"My husband," she choked out around a sob. "I wish you didn't have to go."

"The King calls," Samuel said. "I dare not resist, and with my increased stipend, you may add even more ruffles to your wardrobe," said Samuel, holding out his arms to her.

Amelia stood and melted into him, burying her face into his chest. She did not care if her tears marked his coat. "I do not want ruffles and lace; I want you to stay."

"I am not an indolent gentleman," he said. He cupped her chin and kissed her cheeks, chasing away the tears. "I cannot shirk my duty. I will be back before you have a chance to miss me. You should be grateful for the time you have alone to restore your sanity, and what of your Aunt Ebba? Go and visit her. I know she misses you, or you could visit Patience and welcome their new little bundle."

"And what of our new little bundle," Amelia asked placing his hand low on her stomach.

"I will be back before your time. I promise you."

"Nothing is so frightening with you nearby," she said.

"I promise," he said again. "I will be here—much help I will be," he muttered.

"Will you write to me?" asked Amelia, her voice breaking. His thumbs brushed the tears away as quickly as they came.

"Every day, until everyone else aboard laughs at my fanatical devotion to my wife," said Samuel.

"Good, I hope they do tease you relentlessly."

"Why if they do, I might feel as though I am still here with you."

Amelia slapped him on the shoulder and then put her face against it pulling him close. She breathed in the scent of him as he spoke.

"No one is as sharp-tongued as you, my Amelia," said Samuel with a sigh. "I shall have to settle for second class barbs."

"No one will speak out against the Captain," she said. "You shall miss me desperately."

"I shall," he said.

He took her hand and they walked together to the front door. Amelia wanted to stamp her feet, but she knew she couldn't. She too had a duty to King and Country, and her traitorous limbs moved obligingly, until they stood in the entryway. She wrapped her arms around him and squeezed, memorizing the feel of him, the smell of him, the large protectiveness of him. Samuel kissed the top of her head, her forehead, her nose, until finally coming to her lips, where he kissed her thoroughly. When he released her, she was breathless, and her tears were silent.

He said nothing but lay a large warm hand on

Amelia's stomach as if saying farewell to his child. Her belly was slightly only rounded now, pressing against the fabric of her dress. She would need to order new dresses. Indeed shopping with Aunt Ebba would lift her spirits. "I think I will visit Aunt Ebba," she said.

"Do not distress yourself," he said. "And when I return we will take some time in the country or in Bath."

"Aye, Captain," said Amelia. She laid her hand on top of his and they stayed like that for a heartbeat; two. Then he was gone, out the door with a wave and kiss on her cheek.

She watched him go; then returned to her piano. Amelia played the song she had begun to write just after meeting Captain Samuel Beresford: A song of the sea, of love and mischief, and the sorrow of parting. The sea pulls away from the shore, but it always returns home. She knew how the song ended now. Her captain was gone, but he would be back, and she had a piece of him here with her, always.

CONTINUE READING FOR A SNEAK PEEK OF...

The Baron in Bath ~ Miss Julia Bellevue
by Isabella Thorne

1

$\mathcal{M}$iss Julia Bellevue and her older sister Jane traveled from London to Bath with a large party; all of whom were her sister's friends and not Julia's own. Although the seats were plush and the steeds were swift, such accoutrements could not make the travel pleasant. Julia knew that she should not complain. Her sister's connections, through her husband the Earl of Keegain, meant that Julia was traveling with the Beresfords' party in all manner of comfort, but the three days travel from London felt interminable. She could not wait to be freed from the carriage even if it meant meeting the gentleman who was the main cause of her worry: her intended.

Since most of the *Ton* retired to Bath to get out of the heat and smell of Town, it was easy for two young women of quality to find a party with whom they could travel.

When Julia had asked Jane to hire a private coach for them, her sister had been perplexed. Jane only reiterated that they would be in good company and dismissed Julia's misgivings about traveling with the large group; saying they would be safer from highway men with the earl's coach and several members of the Royal Navy along with their sisters and ladies.

It seemed to Julia that most of the Royal Navy fleet was outside the window of the coach. The men were rather loud, laughing and joking with one another, excited for their summer holiday in Bath. Several had chosen to ride astride and others rode up front with the drivers.

The men made Julia nervous. Their presence only reminded her of the gentleman she was traveling to Bath to meet. Men in general made her tense, and gentlemen in particular, tended to cause her to lose what little poise she had. Perhaps it was her mother's blood which too often seemed to come to the surface and with it, a most unladylike interest in indelicate thoughts.

Although Julia was not much of a horsewoman, she thought the gentlemen looked much happier outside of the coach. She admired the masculine cut of their jackets as they rode. She let her mind wander from one to the other, and although she was already warm in the close confines of the coach, she felt a familiar heat fill her face as she admired the form of one of the men who had loosened his jacket and stood in the stirrups to stretch. Ladies were not supposed to have such thoughts, she admonished herself especially not betrothed ladies.

She tore her eyes away and turned back to the interior of the carriage where her sister was conversing with the other ladies of the *Ton*. Julia brought up her fan to hide her blush, but she also needed it to move the otherwise stifling air in the carriage.

Even her sister Jane's normally perfectly coifed dark hair was clinging to her brow in damp ringlets, albeit neat ringlets. Julia looked like a wilted mess. Both Julia and Jane were brunettes, but that was where the similarity between the sisters ended.

Jane looked like a princess; Julia was more likely to be mistaken for a knight. Jane was regal, whereas, Julia was large and awkward both in form and speech. Jane was ever the countess. She shined at parties. Her words were kind and men sought to please her; women to emulate her. Julia was blunt to the point of rudeness, and often managed to unintentionally insult someone important. Men found her uncouth and she found them overly filled with pomposity.

Unlike Julia, Jane had looked forward to this trip and time sharing a carriage with the other ladies. Julia knew the traveling party would be rather boisterous and she had dreaded the trip before it actually happened. The reality did not disappoint.

Now, Julia sat quietly in the corner of the coach, picking at a string on the plush upholstery while her sister's friends talked around her. Julia would have liked to remain invisible, but it was hard to be inconspicuous when one's breeding and stature were so obvious.

Some said she was an unnatural Amazon. Julia towered above the other women, including her sister. It made her uncomfortable and self-conscious. In an attempt to alleviate this fault she shifted downward in the corner. At least she was sitting in the coach, so her monstrous difference in height was not so apparent.

Before they departed Julia had admonished her sister that under no circumstances was she to try to draw her into conversation with the other ladies, and Jane had reluctantly agreed. In polite company, Julia tended to make one gaffe after the other, so she tried to be silent. Jane was quite the realist and knew trying to converse with her sister in the coach would be a disaster. Julia would have nowhere to flee if she made some *faux pas*. Sometimes however, her tongue seemed to have a mind of its own.

Julia had only a sparse handful of friends herself due to the rumors of her birth, and was really only comfortable speaking with them. None of these friends were with her now, but at least she could look forward to seeing them in Bath – that is if this odious journey ever ended.

She turned her body towards the window and looked out of it again. They were now on the last day of travel, and Julia could no longer ignore that there was a reason for their trip to Bath, other than the summer holiday. The thought made her stomach tie up in painful knots.

When the conversation in the coach turned into a heated discussion over which man was more of a rake: Neville Collington, the Earl of Wentwell or Godwin Gruger, the Baron Fawkland. Julia wanted to sink into the floorboards of the coach. Lord Fawkland, was the very man to which her father had so thoughtlessly betrothed her: the gentleman who caused her trip to Bath to be fraught with such anxiety. Though it seemed, according to the ladies' gossip, that the baron was less than a gentleman. Julia simply bit her tongue and blushed.

She could only hope the other women forgot about her entirely. She slid further down in her seat and wished she could disappear, but she was far too large a girl to even become inconspicuous, never mind invisible.

"I have heard that Lord Fawkland escorted a lady home in his carriage," a blonde friend of Jane's said. She paused for effect, fanning herself. "Without a chaperone."

"It has come to my notice that this was not the first time," the other lady, a pert red-head added.

Julia must have made some noise that drew their attention, for the first woman turned to her. "Is it true then," The blonde asked. "Did your father truly betroth you to the Lord Fawkland?"

The lady's startling blue eyes were fixed on Julia and she found all she could do was murmur.

"Yes."

"Well, he is very good looking," the blonde replied. "In a rather large and over-bearing sort of way. You must admit that."

The second lady tsked. "Oh, dear, you know looks are not everything. The poor girl, how perfectly horrid." She looked sympathetically at Julia. "Is there not some way around it?" she asked.

Jane shook her head at her friends, answering for her younger sister. "My husband, has his solicitors looking into the matter, but he suggested we go ahead as if it cannot be broken."

Julia noted that mercifully, Jane did not go into great detail here amongst near strangers. "But perhaps it can be changed," Julia murmured to herself. At least Jane had asked her husband to check into the matter, even if he offered little hope. Julia reached across and gripped her sister's hand in thanks. Jane smiled at her briefly, but offered no other encouragement.

Julia supposed that her father had planned with her best interests at heart when he made the arrangements for her after his death. Yes, he had left her with a last request, which as it was a last request, it was not a request at all. It was a command. He had betrothed her to Godwin Gruger, the Baron Fawkland, all unbeknownst to Julia, thinking he was a childhood friend. Without a doubt, this was prior to the soiling of Lord Fawkland's reputation. Her sister Jane was initially quite elated that Julia would become a baroness, but Julia did not share her sister's love for titulature.

Julia was not a social person. She could not possibly be a baroness. No. She did not want to marry the Baron Fawkland. Julia and Godwin Gruger had never been friends, even as children. Their age difference had been too great, and Godwin thought himself already a baron. When his father died and Godwin had actually inherited the barony, he came home from the Navy even more cool and distant.

The one time she had spoken with him since Julia felt entirely out of her depth. She had never gotten on well with Godwin, and now if rumor was to be believed, he was a terrible rake. He had not changed from the wicked boy who had broken her dolls; for it seemed he was now just as careless with women's hearts. Everything was wrong with her father's decree. It was Lord Fawkland's younger brother Cedric she remembered. Cedric was much more lighthearted, ever involved in some trick.

Oh why had her father not chosen Cedric instead of Godwin? Julia was nearly of an age with the younger brother, though she must have been about ten when she had last spoken to him. Still she *had* played with the younger brother as a child when Cedric had invited her on his mischievous jaunts. He had even played tricks on the ladies who teased Julia on her behalf. Some of those, she now thought, were quite cruel, but his older brother was over six years her senior and a stranger to her.

If only the words had not also been immortalized in her father's will, an irrefutable document that sealed her fate. Still she clung to the hope that the earl's solicitors may yet find some way to twist the will to her favor, a loophole to slip through.

Julia had given the matter considerable thought. It was not as though she did not wish to honor her father's dying wish, but the terms of the arrangement were entirely unfair, and she knew that if she had had but a moment to confer with him, her father would have changed the conditions. If her prayer could be answered, she would have asked for just five more minutes with her father, but if that prayer would be so granted Julia was sure she would not have used those precious moments to speak of her marriage.

She loved her father, and missed him terribly. Melancholy filled her. She sighed, uncertain how to proceed. Her father had always taken care of such things for her, and although she had her sister to help her, Julia still felt bereft without their father. It was not her sister's responsibility. Nor was it the responsibility of her sister's husband, the earl. She needed someone of her own. Julia wanted a husband, just not Godwin Gruger.

CONTINUE READING....
The Baron in Bath ~ Miss Julia Bellevue
by Isabella Thorne

Made in United States
North Haven, CT
01 July 2022